BROTHERHOOD IS GOING TO THE DOGS.

Praise for *One of These Things Is Not Like the Other*

"This gorgeous existential mystery is a page-turner, a grand novel of possession from beyond the grave in which the nuclear family becomes an opera of identity puzzles. Surprises contend on every page. Father may know, but daddy knows best."
—Robert Glück, author of *Denny Smith*

"D. Travers Scott's new novel is a tall tale like no other, insinuating itself into your psyche much the way the central figure pervades the dreams and actions of his troubled sons. A brand-new myth that crawls inside modern notions of brother-hood and fatherhood as well as the ways masculinity is traditionally conceived against the supposed American ideal of individualism; the book effectively flays alive all received wisdom on these various apprehensions, and it does so from the inside out, in ever-increasingly ugly eruptions from beneath the skin, revealing the shocking bones beneath the torn muscle and sinew of what we call a family. Scott more than delivers on the promise of *Execution, Texas: 1987*."
—Craig Lucas, writer/director of *The Dying Gaul*

"Populated by surreally incestuous brothers and sexy para-psychological polymorphs, D. Travers Scott's latest novel *One of These Things Is Not Like the Other* is a jagged and multifaceted backwater noir, filled with revelation and full of life."
—Stephen Winter, producer, *Tarnation*, *Chocolate Babies*

Praise for *Execution, Texas: 1987*

"Elegantly constructed and very smart…holds more crackly energy than a box of firecrackers."
—Scott Heim, author of *Mysterious Skin: A Novel*

"D. Travers Scott's novel is, in turn, both funny and disturbing…captures the mystery and confusion of an American youth where the search for love is equaled only by the search for drugs. I applaud him."
—David Sedaris, author of *Dress Your Family in Corduroy and Denim*

"Wonderfully evocative, and the characters are the book's great strength…probably the most interesting gay debut novel since Dale Peck's."
—*Melbourne Star-Observer*

"At turns funny, creepy, and frustrated, this book seethes with complex erotic tensions and highlights the strangeness of its middle-America setting."
—*The Village Voice*

ONE OF THESE THINGS IS NOT LIKE THE OTHER

D. TRAVERS SCOTT

ONE OF THESE THINGS IS NOT LIKE THE OTHER

suspect thoughts press
www.suspectthoughtspress.com

Cover image and design by Shane Luitjens/Torquere Creative
Book design by Greg Wharton/Suspect Thoughts Press
Print management by Jackie Cuneo/Little Jackie Paper

First Edition: May 2005
10 9 8 7 6 5 4 3 2 1

Library of Congress Cataloging-in-Publication Data

Scott, D. Travers.
  One of these things is not like the other / by D. Travers Scott.
    p. cm.
  ISBN 0-9746388-6-2 (pbk.)
 1. Identity (Psychology)--Fiction. 2. Fathers and sons--Fiction.
3. Masculinity--Fiction. 4. Quadruplets--Fiction. 5. Brothers--
Fiction. I. Title.

PS3569.C614O54 2005
813'.54--dc22

                                                        2005003754

Suspect Thoughts Press
2215-R Market Street, PMB #544
San Francisco, CA 94114-1612
www.suspectthoughtspress.com

Much appreciation to the following for their help in developing this book: Ellen Blum, Christina Brown, Madeline Crowley, David Eckard, Jennifer Natalya Fink, Dan Garlington, Keith Kahla, Rachel Kessler, Craig Lucas, Mark Mitchell, Valarie Moses, Ian Philips, Larry-bob Roberts, Matthew Swank, Matt Bernstein Sycamore, Brandon VanOver, Mitchell Waters, Greg Wharton, and Paul Willis. Apologies to anyone I've overlooked.

Portions of *One of These Things Is Not Like the Other* originally appeared in slightly different form in *Holy Titclamps*, Larry-bob Roberts, ed.

For Matt

My body no more inevitably united, part to part, and made one identity, any more than my lands are inevitably united, and made one identity…
—Walt Whitman, *American Feuillage*

I turned on the light again and read. I read the Turgenieff. I knew that now, reading it in the oversensitized state of my mind after too much brandy, I would remember it as though it had really happened to me.
—Ernest Hemingway, *The Sun Also Rises*

PROLOGUE

A man walks into a bar. The bartender and two career alkies endeavor to ascertain his identity, struggling against the open-door flood of afternoon sun. Like molten ore into a forge, light pours around the fellow, casting him in silhouette. The sun electrifies his red hair into a billowing halo of flame, a corona burning wildly around his skull. The sun and the hair, the son and the heir.

The bartender gasps. "Jake!"

He releases his grip on the handle, the door slamming shut behind him. With measured steps, he advances toward the mirrored bar until the hanging gas lanterns illuminate his features. The beer company logos etched on their globes inscribe colored scrawls across his face. He is a blond. His eyes are dark.

"Oh, I'm sorry," gushes the girl, flicking her own fair hair out of her face. "I thought you were someone else." She seems to sigh slightly, in relief.

"I'd like bourbon," he instructs her. "Shots of bourbon. Four." He holds up the corresponding number of fingers.

She nods, sets up the shots, and steps back. He strokes a birthmark below his left ear. Sotto voce, he speaks with a sing-song cadence, as if reciting a prayer, a pledge, or a well-worn family tale.

"Once upon a time, one was not alone, but four." He raises a glass and eyes the first brown dose. "For a generation, a regeneration, from sea to shining sea."

He downs one shot. His sallow skin creases as he grimaces at the bitter booze. He drinks two more. "Foursquare, he

15

forswore: we came to be, he came to me," he says, lining up the empties between himself and the final shot.

The bartender frowns, appraising him. She polishes the bar, trying to sneak a sidelong look.

"Yes?" he asks her, just a tinge of threat, a soupçon of seduction twisting his tone, daring her almost.

"I'm sorry." She smiles, pretty, a piercing below her lip catching a glint from the lanterns, her dimples digging shadows. "When you walked in here, you just...you just looked a lot like someone, uhm..." She blushes even, shaking her head. "Someone I didn't want to see," she confesses, casting her glance sheepishly floorward.

"Really?" she hears him say, and she looks up with her best snag-a-tip smile, leaning forward on the bar, bosom manifest but destiny uncharted.

The man looks completely different. With wild red curls, laughing emerald eyes, and a fierce, animalistic expression contorting his dark face, he taunts her, "Of whom do I remind you?"

She jumps, whacking a lantern with the back of her head, and in the vertiginous shadows' swing he is again alien, a passive blond stranger.

OREGON

You're your own man.

Fir branches whipped past the carriage. Palms moist, Jake cradled the messenger bag in his lap, finger-tapping a tattoo along its rubber seam. His phone bag and a portable 8-track player rocked between his feet, jumping with bumps in the road. His lips pressed tight against his teeth.

It's just a visit. You're not going back in time. You've got your own life now, all your own. All on your own. You are your self.

The carriage stopped, and the hired driver rearviewed Jake, eyebrows raised, mouth impassive. The horses panted and rattled their bridles.

What's he waiting for? Jake thought. *Can't believe this town still uses horse taxis.*

The driver jerked his head to the side. Jake turned to look through the passenger window of the carriage, pulling aside the curtain. He held his breath. A gravel road spurred off the highway, twin ruts veering sharply into broody forest.

"He don't let anyone get any closer," the driver called out so Jake could hear. "Remember last time?"

Jake's face flushed hot. He'd never been here before. But he did not correct the driver, merely thanked him and climbed down the carriage running board, setting his bags in the gravel at the side of the road.

The cab left, horses' clip-clops giving way to the hiss of wind in evergreen needles. Jake slung his messenger bag over his shoulder. He laced his fingers through the straps of the phone bag and gripped the 8-track player's handle. He eyed the approach to his father's latest home.

Jake stepped onto the wet gravel, squishing small rocks into the mud. Slick ooze spotted the white leather and orange Velcro of his new running shoes. He shook his head. *Why the fuck did I wear these?*

Jake advanced. Looming conifers congregated around the gravel path, knitting a dark tunnel over him. The highway vanished. No sign of the house ahead.

A banana slug crawled across a red maple leaf. Squatting, Jake studied its undulations. He took a picture of it with the digital camera built into his 8-track player. But that capture wasn't enough. He wanted to touch it. He slid a finger across its glistening yellow skin as when, working at the mortuary, he traced out the flaws on a cadaver's face. He brought his finger to his nose and sniffed. He recoiled with a nauseated expression. Wiping his finger on his jeans and rolling his eyes, he rose and peered down the narrow road, now withered to a pebbly trail, empty before and behind him. He turned back and forth, indecisive. He whimpered, alone in the forest, but no one was there to hear him.

"Jesus!" he said aloud. His voice startled him, and he gasped a tad, taking in a deep breath of the forest, and catching for the first time a scent of wood smoke. He set his shoulders and pushed forward at a faster pace.

The house appeared. A cabin, really. Wood weatherboard. Oddly narrow and tall for such an isolated home, second floor stretching upwards as if in competition with the evergreens. Honey yellow paint faded to bone, cracking and peeling to expose navy scars. Buckling porch floorboards. Mirrored planes of solar panels mounted atop a roof missing shingles. Toolshed and outhouse in back. Garden larger than house.

Brow sweating, Jake approached the house. He scraped his sneakers across the grass until the fuscous mud on each gave way to a glitter-specked, translucent sole. When he'd bought the shoes, back where he lived in West Hollywood, Jake had experienced for the first time the feeling of, *Am I too old for these?* It had leapt past his concern about the expense, asserting itself in his consciousness like a neighbor who'd just moved in, ringing Jake's doorbell with a loud shirt and cheap Syrah. Indignantly Jake had bought the shoes, plus a pair of designer sunglasses, and then gone and had his buzz freshened at the gay rock-and-roll barbershop.

ONE OF THESE THINGS IS NOT LIKE THE OTHER

Shoes sparkling, Jake climbed the splintery porch steps on the balls of his feet to avoid creaking. The door was open.

You can do it. You're your own person now. He entered his father's domain.

The man said, "Now you're here." He didn't turn from his desk.

Jake set his bags by the door. "Did you get my messages...sir? I didn't want to come at a bad time."

"You'd return before too much longer," he sighed. He jabbed a keyboard with his index finger. "I've been preparing." He pushed his mouse an inch. He spanked it with his outstretched palm to elicit a click.

"I haven't seen you in two years, sir." The snug sleeves of Jake's gray V-neck sweater barely covered his wrists; he tugged at them nervously.

His father turned to him and blankly blinked. "You were here only two months ago."

Jake surveyed the house. Familiar handmade furniture, piles of books and papers, taxidermy projects in various states of completion. But something else consumed his father.

Jake Senior climbed out of his chair to kneel before a wall of electronics: smoothly curving glass rectangles of green on black, white on black, and full color; tangled gray cords streaked with sooty grime and wisps of lint, trays of paper in the jaws of black rubber grips, a half-dozen square RFID tags wired like teeth into the open mouth of an 8-track cassette player, minuscule lights of yellow, red, and chartreuse; shiny black-and-steel circles-within-circles of telephone dials, a pair of virtual reality goggles draped over rabbit-ear antennae, digital displays of numbers, bouncing needles of power indicators, the discrete waffles and pinprick grids of speakers, and, jutting out at an angle, a bent coat hanger webbed with aluminum foil.

Now, that's new and different. Jake gestured to the technology mosaic. "They told me about this."

The old man crawled out from under his desk, a curling phone cord in his hand. "Are you already taking more time off from work? Your last visit was quite recent," he said. He reached behind a dusty monitor and patched in the plug. "I remember it vividly," he said, sitting down. He grabbed his desk. He rolled on the squeaky wood chair to another monitor.

19

He clicked his tongue. "Easter."

Jake ran his palm across his shaved scalp. "Ah, no, sir. I'm afraid not. I just got here. I think, I think that was Al- Jake from Alaska who was here at Easter."

His father tossed Jake a raised eyebrow. Jake nodded. "Specificity—doesn't matter," his father said and returned to work.

Jake eyed the mechanical altar. *His new baby. Is the damn thing alive?*

Power cords and cables snaked across the wall like veins and arteries, crawling upward to converge over the balcony rail of the house's lofted second floor. A CB antenna curled against the ceiling.

"I'm Jake from down in California."

The old man sniffed, gingerly twisting a switch. "I've already said that individuality is irrelevant."

Jake clasped his arms behind his back. "I tried to let you know I was coming out, sir. I sent telegrams, faxes, and email, left voice mail, paged you, but I never heard anything back. They said it'd be okay to just show up, so I booked a blimp and...here I am."

The man ran a finger along the cold, black glass of a dead monitor. "Your presence is inevitable. But not my response."

He grabbed an 8-track from a tin bucket under the desk, tangled in unspooled tape from a reel-to-reel recorder, and dropped it back in the bucket.

Jake approached his father from behind. Jake Senior turned his head from screen to screen, tapping mice, pecking keyboards. He clicked his tongue and reached behind a console, a loud chime announcing a reboot. The intensity of his gaze, the focus of his engrossment, never flickered.

I remember that look.

Jake looked at the screens closely for the first time. Direct feeds of weather satellites, news headlines, and download timers pushed onto multiple windows tiled across monitors of assorted ages and makes. Black, beige, and translucent tangerine, even rubberized black matte bodies housed screens flashing icons and scrolling alerts across striped borders and vibrant blue fields. Volume meters bounced on control panels playing audio and video feeds. Chat rooms unfurled in fits and starts under instant messages demanding attention.

"Not your concern," the man warned. He grabbed from under the desk a remote helmet with eyelock goggles and screwed it onto his head, curls of reddish gray hair peeking from under the straps. He waved away Jake.

Moss and moisture disfigured the roof's shingles. Thick morning fog locked a damp chill in the air. Jake shivered with his shirt off, pale freckled chest exposed to the Northwest air. He wished before leaving home he'd taken the time to tan.

"I can employ people for that. They'd do a better job."

Jake twitched at the voice. He pulled nails from between his lips and peered down to the porch.

"What?"

"I don't require your aid. Don't you have affairs of your own, some work you're supposed to accomplish?"

"Yes, but I'm here now, visiting you," Jake said. "This needs to get done, so I'm going to do it. Besides, you're getting it for free."

"Your work will be subpar."

Jake sighed. "I'm sorry, but you don't have us to custom-build for you anymore, so why don't you let me do this work while I'm here?"

Jake stared out at the evergreen-cloaked hills, disappearing into gray blankets. He shook his head. *Can't believe I'm slaving away for him of my own free will.*

"It's not merely effort," his father announced. "Quality is important, as well."

Jake gave in and raised his legs. He slid down the roof, grazing his arm on a solar panel. Wincing, he descended the ladder to his father.

"We're not kids anymore, you know" Jake snapped, rubbing his arm. He caught himself; his eyes widened. His hand rose to cover his mouth, paused, and retreated into his jeans pocket.

For the first time in the two days since Jake's arrival, the man eyed him closely. Jake returned the gaze of his aged mirror. A tall but wiry body with a slight paunch confronted cut pecs and six-pack abs. Cold green eyes stared down a matching pair shielded by contacts, cobalt blue. A curly red beard faced a clean-shaven jaw sporting only a precise strip from chin to lip. More hair, russet gray and curling from under a black knit cap, contrasted a smooth scalp. Profuse wisps peeked from the open neck of his father's cotton henley. The smooth curves of Jake's chest grew chicken-skin, the clammy breeze nipping his razor burn. His father's hands rested in the side pockets of a plaid wool coat. He looked at home in this rural environment, whereas Jake seemed diminished, lessened. His gold hoop earring, bereft of the flash of West Hollywood strobes, hung dull and lifeless under the Oregon fog.

None of the men's differences made any difference. The pout of the full lips, the auburn eyelashes and eyebrows, the white skin, the faint freckles, the hook of the nose, the set of the broad shoulders, the arch of the back, the contrapposto stance—they all remained steadfastly identical, irrefutably familial. No accoutrements or geegaws could affect an effective masquerade. His father's gray hair and haggard creases testified to only time, not difference. Save for age, his father still seemed the fifth quadruplet.

"Holly-wood," he repeated in a sarcastic drawl.

"Yes, sir. Well, West Hollywood—"

"Don't correct me!"

Jake bit his lip. "Jake's in Alaska; Jake's in Dallas. And Jacob's in New York."

The man spat. "Every one of you left, scattered across this country from one end to the other. Ran off to have your own small, particular lives. Left me bereft."

"I'm here, sir."

"Yes, deigning to return to my presence. How long—"

"I'm sorry, but it's not like you get off on—"

"I am speaking!" His father shoved Jake's shoulder. Shaking his head, Jake turned and climbed the ladder.

His father shouted up after him. "Toiled my years away on you boys, and look at the result. Sloth and ingratitude. I don't need you. I never did, yet I worked all those years on you anyway."

Jake crawled to the far side of the roof. *I am not this much of a masochist.* He sat and randomly whacked his hammer against the wood, drowning out his father.

"But you certainly need me. I'm tired of doing all the work for you boys. You're nothing without me. You'll see. My final act."

Jake drew his knees to his chest as a chilly breeze crept in from the east. He looked over at his father's garden. The earth was flat, well tended. Unlike the houses they'd grown up in, this yard sported no memorial tombstone for their mother.

What is the strategy of your aggressive glares deep into the eyes of the boys you fuck? You're not the sort to cavort with your prick somewhere unsolicited; you're far too polite, too cosmopolite of a lad. But in how many ways do you assay to invade some man's intimacy, to fondle his feelings without consent? The hint of connection in sexual machinations you use to manipulate your target soul, the firestorm you exert from your heart to another to get them to astipulate to your goal. You know you can do it; you know there's more than one way to invade a man. Finessing the agile use of your own vulnerability in order to seduce: revealing enough to coax more from them than a feeling bluff. Their affection unwitting and unconscious, yours a hard-hitting affectation of trust. Knowing how to appear to succumb just enough: simulating release and faking abandon to prevent rebuff.

You treasure your emotional bedpost notches: The activist boy crying in your clutches — then cold the very next day. The fellow gasping in shock while you filled him with your cock as if it were his very first lay. The straight ex lured back to your sex. The tough ex-Marine, his whimpers and screams a plea for a harder beating. The boy kissing blue in the tree limbs, as night the dawn was defeating. Sexclub façades of cool melting into coos of "Come home with me." Scorned boys who keep coming back with a metronome's regularity. Attempts to corrupt couples during a threesome affair: fucking one insensate but locking his lover in a deep-eyed stare.

What is it you really want from all of these men? Why can't you scratch that spastic yen? Such gymnastic misbehaviors with promiscuous freaks will never provide the esemplastic savior you seek.

Jake opened his eyes, sighed. He swung his legs over the side of the couch. He blinked and rubbed his forehead. He stared at the floor, another dream of his father lingering in his mind. Looking up, he saw his father, already busy at work at his computers, controlling one with glances from his headset, another with a mouse, another with a keyboard, conducting his symphony — of what? Jake felt confused, jealous.

His father remained married to his electronics all day. Jake worked more on the roof. The men hardly spoke. At supper they came together, Jake facing him across the kitchen table, chewing cornbread.

"You've become rather lazy," his father said. "Too many lumps in the batter. Didn't stir it enough."

They glared at each other. *Deal with it.*

His father set down his fork and said, "Might as well get to work." He pushed from the table and returned to his equipment in the living room. Jake rose from the table and filled the sink with hot water.

Don't know why I bothered, Jake thought amid the din of dishes. *Would've rather seen the old Kentucky house than him. Could've gone all the way back to Texas and had more fun than this. Fucking Oregon. Oh, fuck!*

Jake grimaced at his wet jeans, now dripping sloshy suds. He eyed his father's floral apron hanging unused next to the kitchen door.

No, I don't think so.

He peered into the living room. Hunched over the desk, his father's back was to the kitchen. Jake grabbed a dish towel from the hook under the sink and stepped away from his father's view, wiping his crotch.

Jake called out, "Nice being able to see news any time you want. Instead of having to wait for the newsreels." His father uttered no response.

Jake hung his towel and returned to the dishes. When done, he announced, "I'm going out back."

His father said nothing. Jake picked up his bag from the sofa.

"I've got to call home and check messages." He held up his bag. "I've got a portable phone."

His father turned and eyed him keenly. Jake swallowed and shifted his weight. Held up in contrast to the electronics wall, his phone bag appeared puny. *Hey, it's not the size that matters.*

"You do that, son," his father murmured. "You just do whatever you feel is important."

Jake turned from his father's eyes.

Jake bobbed his head in concert with the steady creak of the rocking chair. The portable phone purred warmly between his legs, cord slung over his shoulder to join the extension slinking through the kitchen window. The antenna swayed with Jake's rocking.

"What?" Jake said, pressing the right side of the headset closer to his ear.

"I said, was it quite the bitch to get there? How was your flight?"

"The airship was only half full, which was sweet. But the drive here from the landing pad took forever."

"Why, where does he live? Is it full-on Egypt?"

Jake stared up at the stars through evanescent cigarette smoke. "No," he told his roommate back in California. "It was kind of a hike but not as bad as some places I grew up." He cleared his throat. "Those were really a bitch."

"Oh, yes. Girl, Theodora told me you once had a little bungalow with a moat around it!"

"No, no." Jake said, chagrined. "In Montana we had to cross a river to get to our place, but it wasn't a moat. We just needed to homestead near a water source. For drinking, and as a boundary between us and the nearest road."

"So it was like a moat."

Jake scowled. "Yeah, but it wasn't round. It wasn't like a fairy tale."

"Five men in a cabin. I know that fairy tale. Rented the laser disc." His roommate hummed lasciviously.

"Oh, get your mind out of the gutter, hon."

"But I'm looking at the stars, sweetie. Looking at the stars."

"Whatever. He wanted it to keep people away, and we couldn't build a bridge over it. But get this: like, instead we built this shack, all camouflaged behind chokecherry bushes. We stored snowshoes there, and crampons, rope, a raft, everything we needed for crossing the river, at any time of year.

"I remember all four of us in a relay line, tossing supplies from the shack to the riverbank, with Dad supervising from the other side. All of us sweaty kids with our wet red hair hanging in our eyes. Then we'd bundle up all our little matching packs, lace up each other's boots, tie ourselves together with rope, then snake across the water in a big line."

"You had to go through that ordeal every time you came or went? Quelle drag. Well, actually, too butch to be drag.

Quelle rigueur."

"Uh, yeah—*quell* my backache."

"*Kwell*, dear? Do you need me to pick you up some more?"

"What?"

"Never mind."

"We didn't do it that often. And we didn't really think about it—you just did what you had to do to get what he wanted. Or what had to get done. If something was broke, you fixed it. If you were cold, you built a fire."

"You really would've made such the bulldagger. Miss Girl Scout!"

Jake smiled, shrugged. "Yeah, but we didn't get any merit badges."

"So this trip there's no building a Bridge Over the River Kwell?"

"No, I just did some work on the roof, which Dad hated, like everything else I ever try to do."

"Oh dear, is the old man being temperamental?"

Jake grinned. "Yeah, he's mental with a temper," he said dryly and made a rim-shot sound: "*Ba-dump chh!*"

"Hmm, yes, no, funny's not your strong suit." His room-mate hummed. "And your dad sounds totally bitchcakes."

"No, he's not as bad as—bitchcakes. It's weird...he spends all his time with these new computers and stuff he's got. He's like the techno queen."

"I thought he shared my loathing of those foul machines."

"He used to. It's weird. It's like this fierce hodgepodge of equipment: a grainy black-and-white surveillance set, a ham radio, a CB radio, all these different-colored monitors and CPUs. It's like he's made a robot baby or something. My brothers warned me, but still, it creeps me out. He just stares at it all day, all serious. Like he used to stare at us."

"How is the rest of the troop doing? You talked to any of the other boys?"

Jake closed his eyes, leaning back in the rocking chair. "They're pretty good," he murmured. "I think Jacob finally had a date. *Something's* keeping him happy these days. But they're all sleeping now, dreaming."

"What?"

Jake opened his eyes. He stopped rocking. "Oh, you know, we're out on the West Coast, it's earlier here, so they must be sleeping now."

"None of them party? Not even the Gotham one?"

"Especially not him."

"I thought you had one in Alaska. Won't he be awake?"

"I don't know!" Jake frowned. "I mean, he and I aren't very close. Probably no." He shifted uncomfortably in the chair, lifting the portable phone base onto his knee. "He's just an early-to-bed type. A clean teen."

His roommate sighed. "Well, hon, I'd love to hear more Tales of the Frontier Family, but I've got to meet Teddy and Georgie. We're going to some porno play tonight."

"Another one?"

"This one has hockey players!"

"Oh, okay. Well, tell them hey."

"Sure, hon, sure. I'll see you Friday."

"I get back Saturday. Don't forget, you're picking me up."

"Right, right, it's on the fridge—ciao!"

Jake dismantled the phone, coiled the cords, and re-packed its case into the bag. The night's quiet filled him with unease. His brows knitted in vague, undirected concern.

The screen door slapped shut behind him as he returned to the kitchen. The house was silent—no gurgling modems or stuttering audio feeds. He stepped through the living room door.

He didn't.

His father hung from a rope attached to the high lofted ceiling. He swung in front of the couch, blocking the view of anyone who might want to watch TV.

He can't.

Jake opened his mouth, tongue twitching. He stared at his father, stepped forward, stopped. He looked around the room, eyes glazed. He closed his eyes, shook his head, rubbed his face, opened his eyes.

Jake rushed to the body. He felt for a pulse at the wrist. None. The man hung too high for Jake to lay his head to the chest, so he pressed his palm against the man's belly, searching for breath, but felt none.

He did.

His touch swayed the body. Mechanical apparatus creaked from the rafters. Jake grabbed hold of the body to steady his father, hugging the corpse, but something hard pressed against his cheek.

Jake turned and saw the bulge from his father's erection, right at eye level. He bolted from the body, face jerking. He wiped his hands on his jeans; his side was wet from his father's cold, sticky sweat, and Jake's own perspiration added to the sheen. Jake brought his palm to his face and smelled his father on his skin; the scent was moist, yeasty, like morning. Tears appeared. Jake ran his hands over his face, scalp, and neck, smelling and tasting.

Fighting to rein in his crying, Jake shuttered his sniffles and whimpers like a boy with a stubbed toe trying to appear brave. He stared at the body, catching his breath, and wiped his face. He reached up in the air toward his father's face.

His fingers clenched into fists, recoiling into hard little apples. He swung wildly at the man, pummeling legs, thighs, and abdomen.

"Fuck you! Goddamn you!"

He ducked and sidestepped the swinging corpse.

Jake jumped back, startled. The ropes and mechanics wheezed. Jake cocked his head as if listening or waiting.

Finally, the phone chirruped. It rang again, a lone protest to the telecom blackout. Jake searched through the electronics hive for a receiver. Hanging on a nail above a wide, flat-screen monitor, he spotted a wireless headset and slapped it on, adjusting the foam over his ears. He grabbed a desk microphone, its green diode blinking, and held its ridged surface to his lips.

"Hello?"

"Holly?"

"Yeah. Jacob."

His brother in New York sounded anxious, breath rapid. "You're with Dad? You're okay?"

Jake eyed the dangling corpse. His father's taste lingered in his mouth. "I'm okay."

"I got a page that I had an email from Dad's address—what the hell was *that* all about? Did you send that?"

"What?"

"The one I just got on my pager. From Dad. I never get anything from Dad so I read it right away. What's all this about humor?"

Jake surveyed the computer array. All screens were black

save one. He inspected the active screen: *There's mail for you.*

"Hold on," he said. Jake bent over the keyboard, hit RETURN. A window opened:

> *I spent my life on you, worked away all my years, risked everything, and it was all betrayed. Spurned and mutated. Perverted and spoiled. I created you, and this is my return. Betrayal by the four of you and now by my body. But these humors are not going to break me down and neither will you boys. My time is up, but my work is not finished with you, no, not at all. My black bile may be rising up, drowning me, but Cronus rises as well. I'm leaving it all, and without me you're nothing. You've never appreciated that, but now I will show you how hard I worked. Now you will know. You will finally appreciate me and my efforts, only I'll be gone.*

"What the hell does this mean?" his brother demanded.

"He just killed himself." Jake collapsed into his father's seat. "He's dead."

"What do you mean by that?"

"Jacob. He hung himself. From the rafters here. While I was doing dishes."

"Our father killed himself while you were washing dishes?"

"That's what I said," Jake snapped.

"What *are* you saying? Is he okay?"

"No, he's *not* 'okay.' He's dead." Jake wiped his mouth with the back of his hand. He squinted, fingers lingering on his chin. "I just got here day before yesterday. I didn't do anything. I worked on the roof and made dinner. He didn't like the cornbread."

"Dad killed himself over your cornbread?"

"Jacob! Um, I've got to—" Violently Jake shook his head, struggling for clarity. "I've got to get him down from there. I've got to call the police." He crooked the phone under his neck and grabbed a mouse. He closed the email window.

"Well, is that it? What's going on? Should I come out?"

"No, don't do that!" Jake frowned. "No, no. And I'm sorry; I won't be able to get anything done until you let me get off the phone. Just let me take care of Dad, let me call the cops, and then I'll call all of us, okay?"

"Of course, there you go, run crying. Bring all of us into this, Holly. Something really serious happens, and you, of all of us—"

Jake bit his lip, scowling. Ignoring his brother's tirade, he bent over and peered at the computer screen. "Do you have another message?"

"What?"

"Do you have another message from him?"

"No, just this one. That doesn't make any sense."

"I do." Jake clicked on the second message, subject heading 'Instructions.' The window blossomed. He read the message aloud:

I refuse to submit to embalming or funeral. Don't waste my money on those scams. Don't insult my countenance with makeup. Don't touch me with your funeral parlor games, Jake. Keep my body. They'll have to do an autopsy, but don't let them keep my body. It's the only real thing, and I've saved it while it's still relatively pure.

Bury me here. It's my land. Don't worry your pretty little head; it's perfectly legal. I've left copies of the state regulations on the hard drive to reassure you—just have to make sure I'm far enough from the well. And remember that gravesites become permanent easement on the property. If you ever sell this land, the buyer has to keep my grave a burial site–he can't ever build over it.

Ignore anything to the contrary that idiot sheriff says.

Here's what you need to do now: Unclamp the release toggle upstairs and lower me down with the winch. Don't drop me.

Go out to the shed for the hedge shears. You'll need them to cut the rope. There's also a zinc-lined coffin and a PVC body bag out there. Ease me into the coffin and make sure to screw the lid completely. Cover the grave with rocks, then sprinkle the entire area with the yellow powder in the coffee can labeled "Fertilizer." It will keep the animals away, permanently.

The laser disc will explain everything. Wait until you hear from my lawyer. Don't do anything stupid until then. I've taken care of everything. You'll all get it all in a few days. Then you'll know the truth.

"Jesus." The phone was silent. Jake tapped PRINT on the email's toolbar. A machine clicked and growled, a rubbery belt clapped, paper shuffled. Jake exhaled softly and leaned back in the chair.

Of course he left me chores.

His brother made a clucking sound of disapproval. "I'm going to call the rest of us," he announced.

"Do whatever you have to do," Jake muttered. "Just tell them to stay out of my hair until I take care of this. You guys wait 'til I can get my work done."

"Well, all right then," his brother said in a tight clip. "If you say so." He cleared his throat. "We'll know when you're ready."

Jake clacked the phone handset into its cradle. Silence reclaimed the house. Lips pressed in concentration, he swiveled the desk chair to face his father. He nodded. *All right. Let's get to work.*

Jake went out to the shed for the shears and bag. Outdoors, he paused and again stared up at the stars. Tiny work lights mounted too high to help? Glimmers of a distant disco? They offered no guidance, but seemed to support some notion of constancy in the world.

Jake returned to the house. He brought a sturdy chair in from the kitchen and planted it below and beside his father. Climbing up, his shoulder brushed his father's feet, pushing the body. Jake flinched, furrowing his bushy red eyebrows, and stood tall on the chair, nearly eye to eye with his father. Chewing his lower lip, he inspected the corpse. He grabbed the rope and tried wriggling his fingers under the cord and pulling, but the slipknot was too tight to release. He stepped gingerly off the chair and walked across the creaking floor to the stairs. Ascending to the loft, Jake hugged the wall. The stairs were open on the side, without a railing.

Upstairs, the roof sloped up behind Jake's head. Whispering drafts brushed the back of his neck. A single twin mattress supported a heap of army-surplus blankets, and a nightstand held a lantern and 8-track cassettes of an audiobook on online research: *Finding Answers on the Global Network.* Thermal underwear, socks, garters, and stocking caps overflowed from a steamer trunk at the foot of the bed. Flush against the far wall stood a three-drawer dresser with a meticulously arranged grooming kit on top: toe and fingernail clippers, curved scissors for ear and nose hair, tortoiseshell brush and comb, and nail file—all parallel. Above hung a cheap piece of silvered glass with a mountain-landscape border.

Beside the mirror his father had mounted a snapshot in a hand-carved wooden frame. Jake leaned closer and peered at the picture of four swimmers. *That's us. That's the creek back behind the Oklahoma house.* Two of them sat on large black rocks jutting from the water; two leaned back into burbling rapids, laughing. *So that's what we all looked like together.*

Jake remembered that day. Their father had returned from town early. He'd brought with him a man. He was supposed to repair the grandfather clock they'd carried across three states. The man had been telling Ally—except he wasn't called that then, they weren't locales then, they were all Jakes, except for the private nicknames when Dad wasn't around: Chairhesty, Crowking, Glowfishie, Koldfist, and more. But the Indie man just called him Jake; he showed them his new instant camera, and surprised them all by taking a picture of the boys.

Their father's fury had exploded. "Don't you dare try to ensnare my sons!" He'd demanded the man leave immediately. He'd whipped the boys with a cedar switch. "Lollygagging in the creek instead of working!" The grandfather clock never got repaired, and they didn't take it with them on the next move, which was not long after.

He got the picture from that day. He saved it.

Jake stared at the photograph. The colors had aged to unnatural hues, and the repetition—their identical features, expressions, and carroty hair—nauseated Jake. Vertigo swept over him. He stumbled onto the bed, breath thin, eyes dry.

The ropes creaked.

Jake put his hand on his chest and sucked in air. *Come on. You've got work to do.* He stood, steadied himself, squeezed sideways between the bed and dresser to get to the loft's edge. With the exception of a central post climbing to the roof, it was as open and exposed as the stairs.

On the support post's interior side, invisible from downstairs, his father had screwed in an intricate pulley system, from which the rope shot up to the ceiling rafters.

Jake yanked the cord. He held it tight with one hand and unclamped the pulley lock with the other. The body jiggled midair. He delicately lowered his father. The body swung, a foot catching on the chair and parting the cadaver's legs. Jake wheezed and raised the body, watching its swing, timing the second descent to avoid the chair. Gently he adjusted the line in his hands, as if ice fishing.

The shoes clomped on the floor, and the legs slid across the wood, shoving the chair away. His dad's ass settled to the floor, as if he were sitting. Jake lowered his father farther, until the head floated an inch off the ground. He eased the rope. A soft bump sounded. He examined the rope stub in his hands. His father had allotted the precise length needed, and its end had been burnt to prevent fray. Jake locked the clamp.

He descended the stairs, again sticking close to the wall. He knelt beside the body but avoided the face, staring instead at the slipknot. He cut the cord with the shears. The stretchy nylon rope had kissed only the faintest line of purple blemishes across his father's neck. Jake stepped over the body and bent to slide his palms into the armpits. He scooped up the 200-plus pounds, and, fearless of tumescence, held his father against his chest. They danced a loping two-step into the kitchen.

He spread his father faceup on the table, legs dangling off at the knee. Jake unzipped the bag and lifted his father's feet into the black vinyl mouth, wriggling it up under the knees. He pushed his father all the way back onto the table. He raised one section of the corpse at a time, sliding the bag under and around the body: thighs, butt, chest, shoulders, head. Jake zipped the zipper. He paused at the face: a face nearly identical to his and his brothers.

Jake looked his father in the eye.

"Hi, Dad," he whispered.

Jake narrowed his eyes. *Broke your neck perfect.* He traced his fingertip along an inverted V-shaped bruise under one ear. *No strangulation marks for you, just this one. Fucking control queen.*

He touched his father's cheek.

You look kind of different.

Hand on zipper, he stared at his father.

You look happy.

Jake zipped the bag, and the face disappeared.

"Oh, I'm sure he killed himself, all right," the sheriff said, leaning against a front-porch column. "People rarely get murdered by hanging. But the Medical Examiner's still got to do an autopsy, you know that."

"Yes sir, I understand." Jake shoved his hands in his pockets. *God, he must think I'm an idiot.* He attempted to change the subject: "Say, do you know anything about humors?"

The sheriff wrinkled his face at Jake. "Well, um, do you know the one about the construction worker who needs a handsaw?"

"No! Humors." Jake nodded, cringing inside. *I am such a—*

"Humors?"

"Yeah. That's what he said in his note. 'Black bile'? He said that's why he was—doing it."

The sheriff nodded, taking this in. "Your dad didn't take to doctors, did he?"

"God, no."

"I didn't think so. I don't think any doctor's diagnosed black bile or anything to do with humors for hundreds of years." The sheriff puffed out his chest and strutted around the porch. "Humors are an old medical system going back to the ancients. Blood, phlegm, yellow bile, and black bile. It's funny he picked that one. Black bile's the one that doesn't even exist. It was supposed to be this nasty stuff that came up from your liver. Makes you sick, crazy. Thought to cause depression. You know, 'black moods.'"

Okay, Jake thought, *I get it. You're not a total hick.* He furrowed his brow and said, "He had plenty of those. That actually makes sense, for him. He wouldn't trust a thing a real doctor would say, but he'd believe ancient Romans." He rubbed his wet eyes.

The sheriff smiled sympathetically. "Greeks, actually," he said. "It started with the Greeks."

Jake nodded at his reflection in the sheriff's sunglasses. "He wasn't really right for our time. Maybe our world. That's why he ended up going away."

The sheriff stepped forward. He put his hand on Jake's shoulder. "Son," he said, "you're not gonna go anywhere soon, are you?"

"No sir." Jake shook his head. *Why the hell do I keep calling him 'sir'?*

The sheriff squeezed Jake's shoulder. "Good boy." He stepped off the porch and headed to his patrol car.

He did NOT just call me 'boy,' did he? Cue the porn music.

Jake straightened his back, tucking in his shirt better, and followed him. "Um, I've got to deal with the will and all his stuff and everything. And you know he wants to be buried here on his land? No embalming or anything? It's legal; he left me a copy of the state—"

The sheriff laughed. "Yeah, I'm aware of the laws in this state." He poked at the grass with his boot tip. "You doing okay out here, all by yourself? It's a ways off the road."

Jake followed. "Yes s— Ah, it's okay; I know my way around."

"I thought you'd never been out here before."

"No, I haven't. I'm sorry," Jake sputtered. "I meant, I know my way around places like this. I grew up in woods and out-of-the-way places. I know woods. Not every forest in the world but, you know, American forests." Jake laughed feebly. "I mean, I haven't studied every single forest across the United States, but I know how they work, you know? Shadows and moss, heat and cool."

"Good things to know," the sheriff agreed.

Jake smiled. "I can actually find my way around with my eyes closed," he admitted shyly. "The sound of the trail, the noise from my boots. Whether the ground is soft or hard under my feet. Animal sounds. He taught us to read and listen to our environment."

The sheriff nodded, stopping at his patrol-car door. "Where d'you live now?"

Jake shifted weight and glanced back at the house. "West Hollywood," he confessed. He offered the sheriff an apologetic shrug.

The sheriff grinned. "Not many forests there. Pretty different 'environment.'"

"Guess you're right." Jake's face clouded, then cleared. "But it's still really the same thing, you know? Being aware of everything around you. I mean, my brothers and I all grew up in rural areas, but even living in cities now, none of us has ever been mugged. I think we're more aware of our surroundings than most people. That's the deal."

The sheriff nodded as he slid into his patrol car. He looked out through the open window at Jake, his head cocked. Jake squatted to the sheriff's eye level.

"So you're okay out here on your own?" the sheriff said. A grin cracked across his face. "I don't need to be coming out to make sure you haven't starved to death? Don't want you going all Donner Party on me."

"But there's no one else here to eat." Jake forced an uncertain laugh, defensive yet flattered. "Oh, you meant—yes, I promise not to cause you any trouble."

The sheriff licked his lips. "Well, we'll see about trouble." He revved his engine.

Jake stood, a confused smile budding. He raised his palm as the sheriff drove away. The car disappeared into the forest. Jake returned to the house, shaking his head.

"What the fuck," he murmured.

Per instructions, the county returned the cadaver when finished. The bagged shape was too familiar to Jake. *I feel like I'm back at work. But I'm not dressing this one up for anyone.*

The county hearse, heading back to the highway, floundered in the mud. Jake abandoned his father on the front porch and went to help push the hearse from its ruts.

Jake returned to the house and spent the afternoon grave-digging. *Glad I got the fag job at work.* When finished, he whacked excess dirt from the shovel, swinging it upside the toolshed, and set the shovel in the corner.

He rolled a wheelbarrow loaded with rocks and the "fertilizer" out to the grave. Jake studied his handiwork: the smooth curve of earth, even and packed. He knelt before it. Sat. Turned around and put his back to the mound. He lay back, stretching across the grave, and spread his arms and legs as if he was going to make a snow angel in the mud.

Jake looked over at the house. *Wonder if you'll still be in my dreams?*

The sky glowed orange, withdrew to blue, then went indigo. Pungent needles of Sitka spruce and a distant promise of rain spiced the air. Trees rustled. The North Star appeared. Jake reached out to it.

"Thanks for the ride home." Jake buckled his seat belt.

"No problem." The sheriff slid into the front seat of the

patrol car next to him.

"And thanks for your patience with all this."

"Least I could do. Sorry I had to drag you all the way down to the station for your statement, but that's procedure." He tipped his hat. "Clackamas County thanks you for your cooperation."

Jake swallowed, his tongue flicking across his lips. He broke into a smile again.

The sheriff slammed his door. "Though, ah, I'm not surprised that you're a real patient guy, having to put up with Jake Senior all your life."

Jake shook his head slowly. "I'm sure you'll never meet anyone like him again in this life."

The sheriff tossed Jake a perfunctory laugh. He nodded and his wide, gray hat brim dipped a shadow across his face.

"Thanks again, sir," Jake said, smiling back.

"Hey, now, you can drop the 'sir' stuff." The sheriff whipped off his sunglasses and tucked them in his chest pocket. "I'm not one of those power-crazy redneck sheriffs. I used to be all big-city like you. Worked back east for a long time before I headed west."

"Oh," Jake said sheepishly. He rubbed raindrops from the stubble on his scalp. "No offense."

"None taken." The sheriff nodded and started his engine. Windshield wipers slapped and screeched across the glass.

"You've been really great, how you've handled all this," Jake said. "When it happened, I thought I'd get taken in and locked up first thing."

The sheriff sniffed. "Well, now, I might've." He checked both ways and eased the police car out onto Pioneer Street. "Especially with a family that's not from here originally."

He leaned back into his seat and stretched his right arm across the seatback.

"I know all the folks around here real well. Most often I can smell a rat soon as we get the call. Hell, half the time I know about trouble before it happens. When somebody starts doing something against the grain, it sets my radar right off."

As he spoke, his fingers flexed and gesticulated, grazing Jake's shoulder.

"Your dad took care of things so it'd be easy for you boys. Real considerate suicide, that one. There's a laser disc he sent to his lawyer. Sort of a suicide note. Makes things pretty clear."

"He said something about that in his email."

"Yeah, the lawyer's waiting to show it to all you boys at once. I got to see it already." He gave Jake a mock-serious look. "'Cause I'm the sheriff, you know." He broke into a grin and elbowed Jake.

"When do we get to see it?" Jake asked.

"Soon." He coughed suddenly. "I think it can only be played one more time, though. Your dad burned the video onto a DIVX disk, like the disposable movies you rent? I think this one only plays three times." The sheriff shrugged. "Suppose your dad's lawyer will get you all the details."

"I can't believe Dad even went in the same room with a lawyer."

"Strange old fart, wasn't he?"

"You don't know the half of it."

The sheriff opened his mouth to speak, but hesitated. His brow wrinkled curiously as he glanced at Jake from the corner of his eye.

"Sure," the sheriff said cautiously. "Well, like I said, the disk clears things up pretty well, and the autopsy sealed the issue. God only knows why he did it. Luckily it's not my job to find out."

"He always has a reason," Jake said simply. "He knows more than we ever will. Even if 'black bile' doesn't make any sense to us, I'm sure there's some real reason behind it."

The sheriff looked askance at Jake. "Really?"

Jake nodded.

"Hm. Hey, look over there." The sheriff pointed to Jake's right. Jake squinted through the rain-dribbled glass.

Three boxy buildings sat in a semicircle past a parking lot. Huge billowing canvases arched over their roofs, stretched across curved scaffoldings.

"That's the Oregon Trail Visitors Center. Oregon City's the Trail's end, you know that? We're the first city west of the Rocky Mountains. When we had the big Centennial, they built that all up to celebrate."

Jake nodded. The canvases sagged, streaked gray in the drizzle.

"See?" the sheriff said. "They're supposed to be covered wagons."

That's one of the tackiest things I've ever seen. Jake turned to him. The sheriff flashed a wide, toothy smile. *Don't laugh.*

"Cool," Jake managed to say.

The sheriff looked back at the road. He stretched in his seat, arching his back. The khaki polyester of his uniform drew taut across his chest.

Jake shifted his weight into the corner of the seat and car door. As they crossed into the edge of town, he shifted three-quarters toward the sheriff. His legs relaxed, thighs unclenching and knees drifting apart, filling the front seat.

The sheriff looked him up and down. "I know it's not much compared to West Hollywood," he said, checking his rearview.

For a second Jake panicked, detecting, he thought, an echo of his father's sarcasm in the way the sheriff said 'Hollywood.'

"But everyone's real proud of what we got here. I am, too."

He diverted onto the rough dirt road leading to Jake Senior's cabin. "Most of the time. Some days, though, I'd kill for a knish."

He chuckled and Jake joined him, although uncertain what the joke was about.

Jake eyed the sheriff. "I kind of miss places like this," he said. "Sometimes. It's nice."

"Maybe you ought to hang out here a while! Take over the ole homestead?"

"This isn't where we grew up," Jake corrected him.

"Right, right, I just meant your dad's cabin."

"Oh. Well..." Jake shook his head with a thin grin. "I can't believe I'm saying this...but that kinda doesn't sound half bad." He tapped the window glass. "Being back in the wild—I never thought I'd say this—it feels—well, not *right*, but...familiar."

"Home again, home again, jiggity jig!"

The car ground to a halt in front of the house. The men sat there. Hand on the gearshift, the sheriff studied the steering column. Jake rested his fingers on the door handle but glanced down at his feet.

"You, ah, you—" Jake stammered, jerking his head toward the rickety cabin, "you want to come in for a beer or something?" He looked back at the sheriff and discovered him smiling.

"Well," the sheriff said, "you're certainly friendlier than

your dad."

Jake met the sheriff's eyes. "Dad and I only looked alike."

"Well. All right, then."

The sheriff tilted back his bottle and swallowed. "It's something, you know," he said. He shook his head and rapped his knuckles against the kitchen table. "At first I didn't notice it, what with your head all shaved and that little Brazilian of a beard and all, but you do really..." He narrowed his eyes at Jake.

"Yeah, I know." Jake coughed. "It's the same with the rest of us. Except for being younger, we all look like him. And, so, of course, we all look alike. And so, of course, we all try as hard as we can to all look different from each other."

He scratched his beard-strip, then caught himself. He shot the sheriff a self-conscious smirk and shrugged. "Maybe more like we're just trying to not look like him. Dad had us when he was twenty-one, so we're about the same age we first remember him being. Maybe we're all afraid of looking in the mirror tomorrow and seeing him. Except maybe Ally."

"That one of your brothers?"

"Uh, yeah." Jake took a big swig. *With brothers like him...*

"You close?"

Jake choked on his beer, sputtering froth onto his chin. The sheriff leaned forward a degree, as if he was about to wipe Jake's face clean, but he restrained himself.

"Ahm, uh—" Jake wiped the beer across his sleeve. *You don't want to know the whole answer to THAT.* "He's just like Dad. Same big beard, same rural lifestyle. Built a cabin by himself up in Alaska. Hunts and fishes, same old story. Except he's really more Dad than Dad. You know how Dad could talk all educated and snotty? Ally just sounds like any mountain man. He's got Dad's life but a different outlook."

"I thought you were all named after your dad?"

"We are, but we have nicknames—you can understand why. 'Ally' is short for Alaska; 'Dal' is short for Dallas. They call me 'Holly' for Hollywood. We used to call Jacob 'Ennie,' but he doesn't like that now."

"Ennie?"

"Short for 'Enwycie.' N-Y-C."

"Ah."

Jake screwed up his face in thought. "We've all moved all across the country. We've got different lives, jobs, even accents, sort of. Dal sounds all Texas and even speaks some Spanish. Jacob's sounded different ever since he started medical school, but it's less of an accent and more of an—attitude. Anyway, we've all tried to become as individual as possible. We just want to be single men."

"So no marriage?"

"What? Oh. I—" Jake bit his tongue. "No, I'm not married."

"Mm-hmm. Me neither. Not anymore." The sheriff contorted his face into a mask of mock tragedy, and they laughed. "How about your brothers?"

"Dal has been living with his girlfriend for about a year. I can't imagine who would put up with Jacob. Ally never will."

"So you're not rushing in to anything," he said. "That's good. Young marriage can be a big mistake. Trust me on that one." The sheriff exhaled loudly, shaking his head, and grabbed his beer. "My daughter's the only good thing that came out of mine."

"I'm not going to get married. And—" Jake licked his lips nervously. "None of us will have kids."

"Now, how can you say that? Kids're great, and, besides, even with all the rubbers and pills in the world, you can't always plan 'em." The sheriff ran his fingers through his slack, sandy hair. "From the day they're born until the day you die, they do what they wanna do."

Jake looked at his feet. *Fuck it. Why not tell him?* He squared his shoulders against his chairback. "Well, yeah, actually. We can't have kids. When we were about twelve, we all got phosphorus poisoning. Dad said it must've come from this old factory near where we lived. He said we must've gotten in digging around where one of their waste dumps was."

Jake sucked on his beer. "Phosphorus causes, ah, testicular degeneration." He looked hard at the sheriff. "But everything works, you know. I can do everything. I just won't ever have kids. Don't want 'em, anyway." He drank his beer.

The sheriff reappraised Jake. "Well, some would think you're lucky. It's a hassle having to worry about kids every time you fuck. Will the rubber rip? Is she really on the pill? One night of fun can cost a lifetime of responsibilities. It's worth it, though, don't get me wrong."

"It's not responsibility I'm afraid of," Jake said huffily.

A low breath escaped the sheriff's lips. "I see."

Jake forced out a brusque laugh. "You know, since we all look alike, and we all look like him, this woman once said we must've not even had a mother, that Dad must've found some way to reproduce himself. I looked up 'parthenogenesis' in our homeschooling books. That's—"

"Asexual reproduction."

"Right, except it starts with a female, so... Anyway, that's one reason I don't visit a lot. Wherever he lives, everyone in town always looks at me funny, recognizes me as the son of that local freak that lives out in the woods. They steer clear of me like they steer clear of him."

The sheriff rubbed his forehead; his flaxen eyebrows stood at attention. "Guess everyone did give your dad a wide berth."

Jake nodded grimly. "Smart move—you just had to look at him to know he was bitchcakes."

The sheriff chuckled bemusedly, but his smile faded. "'Scuse me?"

Jake's face clouded, brow furrowing. "He's so, you know, different. Not like other men. One look and you can tell he knows what you're thinking, and then some. He's always known things he shouldn't've known." Jake drained his beer.

"Really now?"

"You'd be surprised," Jake said. "If you really knew everything that man's capable of." He bit his lower lip, staring at the empty bottle in his hand.

The sheriff scratched the side of his nose. "So," he said brightly, "how come all of you all never ended up on TV? Seems four identical twins and an identical father would've been all over TV. Wasn't he proud of you four boys?"

"Oh yeah, especially when we were young. Dad thought there was something real extraspecial, practically sacred about the number four. He always talked the four elements, the four compass points, our four limbs, the four legs that make a table solid, a perfect square—"

"The four humors."

"Exactly. And he didn't want to cheapen something so universally significant. He didn't want us corrupted by society," Jake said simply. "He hated that stuff. We never had a TV or anything. We had a text-messaging ham radio, but only for emergencies. He hid the batteries in his bedroom with his liquor and ammo."

Jake glanced upstairs at the loft. "He wanted us to completely avoid the outside world. He wanted us to know only the four of us and him, depend only on the us five, and basically be our own world. He dressed us alike, gave us the same hatchet-job haircuts, homeschooled us. We never questioned it for the longest time. We thought towns were sick places, like hospitals or quarantines. He made us think people lived there because they weren't strong enough to live on their own. We thought we were normal."

Jake's gaze crept across the surface of the table. *Don't get all sloppy and tell him everything!* "Like, we thought everybody could feel each other." *Shit, too late.*

"What?"

"In your head, we thought everyone could feel each other." Jake picked at his beer label with his thumbnail.

The sheriff raised an eyebrow, still smiling. "What do you mean, you guys psychic?"

"Not like Dad was," Jake said, shaking his head.

The sheriff blinked, still propping up his smile.

"We're more like—it's like this background hum in your head, like a shadow-chorus of my brothers' feelings. We used to think everyone experienced it, except with their parents, of course. He could keep us from feeling him."

"Don't think I'd want to get inside your dad's head," the sheriff said with a sad smile.

"He wouldn't have let you," Jake said. "We tried testing his powers. When we were teenagers, we started sneaking away at night, just one or two at a time. Each time we'd go farther from the house. There was a service station down the highway a few miles, with magazines, TV, and a video game. They were one of the first to switch to electric, and that'd be good for us later. So one or two of us would go there, and the others would stand watch outside my father's room, and we'd feel their fear if he woke up."

"That was handy," the sheriff said as he helped himself to another beer from the icebox. He held one up for Jake, who shook his head and said, "No, they're too warm."

"Run out of ice?"

"Yeah, it all melted. I could find the number for Dad's ice guy. Who delivers around here?"

The sheriff shook his head. "No one. Your dad came to town for it. I could drive you—"

"Thanks, no, don't go to the trouble. I'll just stick 'em in the creek tomorrow to cool." Jake looked up at the sheriff, catching him with his mouth clamped around the neck of the beer bottle, trying to unscrew the cap with his teeth. Jake grinned quizzically, and the sheriff spit the cap into the sink.

"Damn imports." The sheriff laughed. He returned to the table and sat close to Jake. "So your dad just knew whatever you boys got up to? Guess most parents do have that ability. I like to think I do."

"Except almost as soon as we started going to the service station, Dad knew about it, even though he slept through the whole night. He'd just know the next day. He'd just know.

"We had about a year of fighting with him, getting caught, being locked in the attic, being tied down to our beds at night. One of us finally got back to the station and asked the man there for help. At first the social worker tried to take us back home, but they decided pretty quick we were better off away from him." He grinned sheepishly.

"We all ended up working at that service station. The owner and his wife, they showed us how to work the rechargers, and that was our first job. Not a lot of people knew how to work them then, so it gave us an advantage. Made up for being homeschooled.

"So they let us fix up their old barn. After a year we were legally emancipated. It was nice. We could all work together, and the house was far enough outside of town, we still felt safe. But we kept on exploring the world more and more, and discovering who we each were. But even then, we always felt Dad watching us. We knew he knew what we were doing every day."

Jake looked up at the sheriff expectantly, as if challenging him.

The sheriff took a drink from his beer. "Well, yeah, like you said, he seemed to know a lot."

Jake nodded his head. "Dad knew everything!"

"Yeah," the sheriff said, appraising Jake. "Around here sometimes, ah, sometimes someone's Super-8 would crap out, or they'd cancel their satellite subscription, and the next day Jake would come calling to see if he could buy the scrap. And folks would swear they hadn't told anyone."

"That's so Dad! He knew little things that could help him out, and he knew secrets, secrets that gave him power over people."

The sheriff looked keenly at Jake. "Yeah, well, Jake, you know—" He blew air between his teeth. Jake leaned closer across the corner of the table toward the sheriff, meeting his eye.

"I never told anyone this, and I wasn't going to tell you, that's for sure, but—he did know things." The sheriff leaned in closer as well. "Other things. One time we, ah, we had an unsolved murder out here—little girl gone missing. And I didn't have lead one. Not a clue worth shit. I was going crazy at the station one afternoon working the case—trying to put pieces together. Hell, I was trying to come up with any pieces at all. I got so frustrated, I went over to the barbershop for a shave. I was in there, sitting in the chair with a razor to my neck, and your dad walks down the sidewalk outside. He stops right at the barbershop window and looks in, right at me. Then he looks down at this local guy in one of the waiting chairs. This guy sitting with his back to the window. Jake looks right down at the guy, then looks back up at me. Then he nods, looking me in the eye the whole time. Then he walks off.

"The barber saw, but he just laughed at crazy ole Jake. But as he finished me up, I realized that man waiting his turn, he was the one that had killed the little girl. He wasn't related to her. No one would've ever thought of suspecting him. But as soon as I got back to the station I started working on him as the prime suspect. Didn't tell anyone. Called in some favors." The sheriff leaned back in his chair, arms across his chest, climactic. "And they found her in his cistern, all wrapped in plastic."

Jake nodded.

"Don't know how much your dad knew, or how he knew it. I suppose I should've investigated him as an accessory but, ah—" The sheriff peered at Jake, tongue twisting for words. "But I didn't do that. I, ah, felt like I owed him one for helping me with the case. So I steered clear."

Jake slapped the table. "That's my dad! Amazing."

"Well!" the sheriff said, scratching his thighs and pushing

up from the table. "Luckily he was also very thorough. You'll see. That laser disc lays everything out just perfect."

He stood up and gathered the empties off the table. "It's a good thing, too. I would've been pretty suspicious of you." He gently clocked Jake's shoulder with one of the bottles. He crossed the kitchen and set them in the sink.

"Son comes to visit for the first time in a long while." The sheriff turned to Jake. "Man who normally lives alone for months at a time apparently decides that's the perfect time to hang himself." He advanced across the kitchen toward the table. "Crusty old loner just *happens* to know exactly how to hang himself just perfect to avoid pain and damage to his body. Son who just *happens* to work in a funeral home."

The sheriff stopped, standing right beside Jake. He hitched his thumbs right under his belt, and his buckle glinted near Jake's cheek.

"Sure didn't look good. But like I said, the laser disk explains everything. And I made a few calls to keep a lid on publicity. I'm sure you boys don't want it, and this town certainly doesn't need it, after all that business a few years ago with the little girl. Jesus. Anyway—the lawyer said he'd be giving you a call right away." He smiled. "And call me if you need anything, at the station. I'm working nights this week, filling in for a gal on maternity leave. But they can message me during the day. Don't be afraid to give me a call."

Jake looked up at him. "Thanks."

The sheriff kept smiling. He clasped Jake's shoulder.

"Not at all," he said. The men stared at each other. The sheriff's thumb crept up the back of Jake's neck.

Jake opened his mouth. He closed his eyes. The sheriff pulled him close, pressing Jake's face against his stiff uniform. His hand grazed the top of Jake's fuzzy scalp. *Well, all right, then!*

Jake released a long, drawn-out sigh which dropped lower, down past the range of mere breath, taking on vocal resonance, a whoosh of air that uncurled and stretched out like a sunning cat, then suddenly curled and transformed into something more like a whimper.

"Good boy," the sheriff whispered, kneading Jake's shoulders. Jake nuzzled his chest. *Uh, yeah.*

The sheriff reached down to the hem of Jake's T-shirt and

dragged it up over his head, giving him a moment of claustrophobia. The sheriff ran his hands over Jake's pale, freckled back, and this time Jake did not consider his lack of a tan. Arms circled Jake's shoulders and squeezed, bristly hairs against the nape of his neck. He lifted the boy up.

Standing face-to-face, he cupped Jake's chin. Jake's eyes darted away.

"Hey, boy," the sheriff murmured. "Come on, look at me. Look at me."

Jake's eyes settled and met the sheriff's.

"That's not so bad, is it?"

Jake shook his head without breaking the gaze.

"You been with men that could look you in the eye?" the sheriff asked.

Jake shook his head.

The sheriff nodded. "Yeah, I know all about that. That's why I moved out here." He smiled warmly at Jake. "Maybe you should've given women a chance."

One hand slid down to his lower back and the other circled the back of Jake's neck. He pulled him into a kiss, slow and deliberate. He never closed his eyes.

Jake broke the kiss, wrapping his arms around the sheriff. He nosed around the man's neck, whimpering.

"Yeah," the sheriff whispered. "Let me take care of you, boy."

"Fuck, yeah." *Did I say that out loud?*

The sheriff's hand slid down deeper, burrowing behind the waist of his jeans, cupping the rising curve of his ass. Jake's knees weakened, his hard-on pressed against the sheriff's thigh as he slumped lower. The sheriff tightened his grip and pulled the boy up. "Don't go away from me," he growled. "Stay. Right. Here."

Jake nodded. This was different from other older guys who'd tried to play tough with him, growling porno-talk and presuming dominance. Jake had usually yawned and walked away, or, better yet, flipped them and fucked them silly. No, not silly. Hard. Cruel. Slamming into waxed asses with little lube and no easy entry. Taking them and feeling good about it. Fucking them over for thinking they could fool him.

But now, in a scenario straight out of a porno script — making out with a sheriff, fer chrissakes! — he was playing the part instead of bucking the trend. He nuzzled his buzzed scalp along the underside of the sheriff's chin. He turned up and took in his tongue, gray blond stubble abrading his cheek as they kissed. The sheriff's fingers moved 'round front, pushing down past the seam of Jake's overdesigned underwear, touching the curly red bush, scratching, stroking, then closing around the thick, hard base of the shaft.

And Jake saw faces. Faces of his brothers, or his father, who could tell? He saw eyes, not their family's green eyes but cold white blue eyes, eyes that he'd seen somewhere before, animal eyes.

Jeans crumpled and shoes skittered, tossed across the table, knocking over the lone remaining beer bottle. Amber liquid dripped down—*splat!*—to the floor and pressed against the back of the sheriff's open shirt, but the polyester absorbed no brew.

The moment came, that moment, that second all fags foresee and yet fear: the comparison, the show-me-yours-show-you-mine, the doctor-play pinnacle when competition faces fantasy, and he whom you must kill is he whom you want shoved deep up your ass.

The sheriff was bigger.

And it was in his mouth, and he was gagging and trying hard again to breathe through his nose like you were supposed to. But his nostrils gathered in acrid funk, sharp sweaty metal-stink that, like so many men of the past year, was not familiar.

"Hey—where'd you go?" He wriggled around to face Jake. Looking at each other, they laid on their sides, naked on the dusty wood slats of the cabin floor.

"Huh?"

"Lost you there for a bit it seemed."

"What do you mean?"

He cupped his palm around the base of Jake's skull. "I like someone to stay with me when we're together."

"I was just getting into it."

He stared at Jake with a faint, fond smile, but the lines around his eyes looked less weather-beaten and more beaten-down. "I know," he said. "Look, maybe this isn't right. Maybe this is too much too soon."

"No," Jake said. He sat up on the floor, cross-legged. "No, I'm glad you're here with me."

He joined Jake sitting, and rested his hand on his knee. "I'll stay here tonight, with you, even if we don't do anything."

"You will?" Jake's red eyebrows raised above his nose in a suppliant expression, softening his countenance so that, even with the shaved head, he resembled less a convict than an orphan.

"Sure."

Jake turned around and leaned back as the man wrapped his arms around him. "There's a, there's a bed here, but it's his. I slept on the couch."

"You got some blankets?"

Jake nodded.

"Then we can just stretch out right here."

Jake smiled. "Maybe by the fire would be nicer."

The electronic purr of the lawyer's car faded away, displaced by the blustery storm brewing outside. Wind surrounded the cabin. The sheriff had left that morning, and left Jake his number. Now Jake was alone with his brothers.

His brother in Dallas pecked at a computer keyboard, scrutinizing his screen. Occasionally he stroked his mustache with a slow, delicate gesture. He sat at a kitchen table, harshly lit by an overhanging brass lamp. Decorative straw baskets and place mats hung on the wall behind him.

His brother in Alaska brooded in an adjacent window, full beard and plaid wool coat, a younger mirror of their dead father. A stuffed wolverine head, mounted to the cabin wall behind him, glared over his shoulder.

His brother in New York, still wearing his blue hospital scrubs, sat patiently in the lower right quarter of the screen, polishing his thick, black glasses. He'd parted his dyed-black hair on the side and slicked it back as much as the curls would allow. A shower curtain and kitchen shelves loaded with dishware and books cluttered the frame behind him.

Jake flipped the goggles down over his father's helmet. "Okay," he said. "We're all here."

"So it was really cancer?"

"Holly, what the hell is that?"

"And he never even went to a doctor."

"Yeah, he was never diagnosed. He just knew. And it's an eyelock helmet. It tracks my eye movements then Bluetooths them to the computer to control it. Dad had it, and the sheriff showed me how to work it."

"He just knew."

"You look like a total chode."

"Fuck you!"

"Lay off him. We don't know what he's been through."

"Uh, hello? Yes we do."

"Holly got himself in the wrong place at the wrong time, but it could have been any of us."

"Can't believe we've got to give away everything."

"*I* have to donate all of it! The church here is already expecting it all."

"Then what are we here for? Damn, I spent all last night getting this mess set up."

"It clears us of any suspicion. Which is strangely considerate of him."

"I put all the instructions in my blog, and the software is idiotproof. A six-year-old could run a video chat."

"Fuck the software, you should've just gone—"

"Enwycie, don't go all bitchcakes on us."

"'Bitchcakes'?"

"It's a gay thing, you wouldn't understand."

"Hey now, y'all, I was out working all day at the garage. I don't need to be coming home to this."

"'Jacob.' And it's not just the will. I'm talking about this whole setup. Us having to do this all synchronized. These damn DIVX disks. It's so anal, and it's just so like Dad."

"You're one to talk, control queen."

"Being anal and controlling will make me a good doctor."

"*'But that tree is full of monsters!'*"

"Ha-ha, very funny."

"The lawyer and sheriff both said it would help keep us from having an inquest if we follow the will exactly."

"Like good little boys."

"You all know he's like watching on some closed feed."

"Yeah, of course. Dad keeps an eye on us from the grave."

"Look, is everybody ready?"

"Yeah," they sighed in unison. Each turned profile in their video frames. Jake turned to the electronics wall. His father had already wired a DIVX player and monitor adjacent to the webcam, sparing Jake an assembly project. He looked at the onscreen control until MENU turned yellow. He blinked twice.

The disk spun, clicked, hummed. A blue field blinked into a navigation window of white-on-black text. It had two choices: *Will*, which they'd already seen with the lawyer, and *Boys*. Jake blinked for *Boys*. He looked at PLAY.

He jumped. His father was sitting exactly where Jake sat now, in the office chair before the electronics wall. Jake looked over his shoulder, where the camera must have stood then. Jake returned to the screen. The aged, hairier version of himself leaned forward. The elder Jake bent and scrutinized an accordion-folded computer printout.

"Well, well," he said. "I hope you've enjoyed all the legalities, but now I have something more I want to share with you boys."

His voice echoed through the four video feeds, looping onto itself and creating feedback whines. Jake's eyes darted to turn down the volume on the other windows.

"I spent my life working on you boys. You know that. I did everything to make you powerful beyond men. Not one of you was up to it. None of you took advantage of my care and nourishment. You strove vainly to become different people, different from each other, different from me. Four legs can't go in four different directions. You pissed away your very strength. Pissed away the most important thing I gave you. I gave you life, and now mine's being taken away.

"But I'm not finished. I have one more thing to teach you. Gratitude. Appreciation. Respect. Call it what you will, I know how to make you finally value what I gave you. And you will rue its loss. I'm leaving this world, and consequently yours will fall apart.

"But I've a going-away present for you. Something that will make you finally appreciate me, and what I did. What I could've taught you to do if you'd been willing to work hard enough."

Jake leaned forward in his seat. Each brother froze in his tiny window.

"One of you is not my son.

"One of you was not of the woman who died when the others were born, when they killed her, when they spurned her from this world that she was too good for anyway.

"One of you is the offspring of a woman named Brett

Ashley. She lives in Brooklyn. Gravesend, to be exact. Go discover what she has to say about all this."

Their father settled back in his chair, smug. "Surprise." He gazed at the camera, as if relishing the shock on his boys' faces. He chuckled and shook his head slowly as static glitches scarred his face.

"But which of you is it? Which of you is the outsider, the alien? And how come none of you knew until now? Why couldn't you tell?"

Reaching toward the camera lens, his palm paused in the upper left of the frame. He bent down and peered close into the electronic eye.

"Now," he whispered, "perhaps you'll fully appreciate all that I am, and all you could have been, with only a little— effort! More perspiration could have fulfilled your aspirations; except, of course, you didn't even have those."

The video went blue.

Not one boy moved, each stared at his offscreen screen.

Jake removed the helmet. He looked at his hands folded in his lap. A thud sounded from the front porch, and he flinched. Storm winds slammed the screen door. Rain splattered the window. Jake looked over his shoulder. Lightning flashed through kitchen windowpanes, casting a cross of shadows across the now-useless icebox.

Jake glanced back to the computers. Muffled thunder rumbled. His brother in Dallas typed busily, his gaze focused inches below the video camera. His Alaska brother, beleaguered by the arguments of his New York brother, held his head in his hands. Jake turned up the volume:

"I think I read about Gravesend in this wiki on local history. It's this old colonial town, settled just after Jamestown and the Pilgrims. But then it became Brooklyn. God, how could one of us be from *Brooklyn*?"

"I want to watch it again."

"Didn't you pay attention?" murmured his brother in Alaska. "They're limited playback."

"Holly? Is one play all we get? Don't you usually get three or five? Hello, Holly?"

Jake looked into his camera, face clenched in confusion. "Sorry. What?"

Jacob rolled his eyes. "One play is all we get from these?"

Jake bristled.

Alaska gazed fixedly offscreen. "One chance is all you get in life."

"Our woodsman is now a philosopher?"

"Well, actually," Jake said, "the disk was made for three, but the lawyer and sheriff have already each watched it. That was the last play." He cleared his throat. "Kwell drag."

"What?"

"How can they do that?"

"Well, that's insane," Jacob muttered. "I'm going to futz with mine again."

"Hey, I'm the one who talked to the lawyer, remember? I'm the one stuck with everything here in Bumfuck, Oregon. Jacob, you don't know—"

"Oh well, thank you very much—"

"I'm sorry, but, I am the one who's had to do all the work, slaving away out here and no one even asks me—"

"Aw, come on now—"

"Yeah, we didn't even get a chance to come out—"

"'Monsters run faster in winter!'"

"No funeral—"

"Y'all couldn't've paid me to come out—"

"Hey!" Jacob waved his hand at the webcam. "Did anyone think to make a dub?"

Jake shook his head. "Wouldn't matter if you tried. I told you—"

"Yeah, he already told you—"

"Some sort of piracy protection's built into them. The lawyer said Dad had been working on the laser disks for months, sending his original out to professional companies that could do this."

Heads shook in familiar amazement. His brother in Alaska raised a finger.

"What about—that lady?"

Jake looked sharply at his webcam. The small white orb stared back, lens black and unblinking like a shark's eye. Jake opened his mouth, closed it. The storm outside roared.

"Delusional," Jacob muttered. "'Humors'!?"

"Maybe not," Dal said coolly. He peered at his monitor and circled slow, graceful arcs with his mouse. He clicked and double-clicked. He squinted, eyes racing across his screen, and cleared his throat. "Brett Ashley, 1764 Granite Lane, Gravesend, New York. She's real."

"That doesn't mean shit," Jacob grumbled. "He—"

Dal continued, not looking at them. "Can't hear or see you right now, so just hold a sec, okay? I've got to check something." He bustled about with his keyboard and mouse. An electronic screech bleated from his audio feed. Alaska winced.

"Hope y'all can hear that," Dal said. "Got the speakerphone way up as it'll go."

Jake looked at his brothers.

"What the hell is he doing?" Jacob asked, shaking his head.

"Relax," sighed Ally. He and Jacob stared at their screens, as did Jake.

"Here I go." Dallas tapped his mouse. A series of jerky clicks and whirs commenced: a phone dialing. Jake grabbed his mouse and muted the other windows. He expanded the Dallas window to full screen. The picture broke into large digital squares—elemental components of the image.

The phone rang. Again.

"Hello?"

An older woman's voice.

"Excuse me, um, Brett Ashley?" Dallas frowned.

"Yes, this is Brett Ashley. How can I help you?"

"Sorry to bother you," he said steadily.

"I'm afraid this isn't a very clear connection."

"Yes ma'am, I do apologize. Ah, listen, excuse me, but, do you happen to know a Jake Barnes?"

Jake held his breath.

"Or his boys with the same name?"

The silence continued.

"You will not contact me again. None of you four. Or I will involve the authorities."

Her line severed. Dallas looked away from the screen, rubbing his eyes. Jake reduced his window. All four were silent for a long, pregnant moment.

"She knew our name," Dallas murmured. "She knew us."

"That don't mean anything," Jacob grumbled. "We're all brothers. Look at us!"

"Sure it does! She knew who we were! Even if Dad was just testing us, she does have something to do with us. We've got some kind of history with her. Something besides just Dad and the four of us."

"I don't have time for this." The window from New York collapsed into a solid gray plane. *Connection terminated.*

Dallas jerked his head toward where the webcam was perched atop his monitor. "I'm going to search her."

"How come she knew us?" Alaska said. "We never lived in Graveyard. Brooklyn. Holly? Holly, what does this all mean?"

"I don't know!" Jake snapped.

"Crap, I gotta free up some memory to get search images, too." Dallas' face was set with the thrill of a challenge. "I'm gonna see if I can find anything about us in Gravesend, or her here in Texas. Maybe she has some connection to that pisspot we were born in. Maybe down in New Garton. I should haul out my maps, too. I'll send all y'all anything I find." His window grayed.

Alaska nodded his head. "Must've been when we were really little," he offered. "Holly—maybe it's you or me!" Alaska's eyes lit up. "Maybe we're not brothers!"

Jake glared at him. "I don't care if we are or not," he hissed. "I don't think—we should be doing this. I mean, it seems—Isn't this what Dad wanted us to find? I mean, it felt like he was setting us up for this."

Alaska picked his webcam off the table and cradled it in his hands like a baby chick. He peered down into it, cooing soothingly to his brother. "Holly, this is us we're talking about. This is who we really are. We gotta follow up on it."

A garbled howl sounded faintly through Alaska's connection. He looked back over his shoulders. "That's the dogs. I gotta check on them." He turned back to the webcam. "We'll talk real soon." He smiled at his brother, eyes wide with hope. "It's all going to be okay now." He looked about for a moment in confusion, then gave the webcam a quick yank. His window grayed.

Jake hit the furthest upper-right button on his keyboard. *Are you sure you want to shut down your computer?* Jake moused the cursor arrow over the SHUT DOWN button and clicked. The conference application collapsed. The screen blacked out. *It is now safe to shut off your computer.* Jake did.

Fuck. Nothing is the same now.

Congratulations on your successfully protuberant pecs. Truly, I'm so proud of you and your sex. The shaved head, the brave beard. That sheriff obviously was smitten with them. In awe of your style. Desperately titillated. In fact, son, you are a star, an urban bohemian success story, a gory allegory of sexual attraction. Baby it's you, my sweetness and light; it's all true, so suitable and right. You're so cute and able at cocksucking delight.

Mm-hmm.

Yes, sonny is a sexy little faggot honey, such a physically distingué youth. All the big boys are desperate to lay you. Papa's immensely proud of his penultimate little slut. Spreading butt far and wide for the West Hollywood tribe's elite, the crème de la crème of the calf implant and liposculpture clique kneeling at your feet. Daddy never got to get fucked by a man with belly fat carved and tucked into six-pack abs. You know, Jake, I'm so proud of your gymnasium and you. You've made all of my dreams come true.

Yet you can't leave well enough alone, can you? You're bamboozled as to why your pushing, striving, and struggling yield zero. Every sexual success you bleed to achieve is revealed a game in which none else have partaken. Only after you score do you discover: you've been banned from play; the teams have called it a day; the referee has left the stadium; the coach, left you forsaken.

But don't fret, pet. Of course you already know this, I'm sure, and I say it without regret: Yes, you always were my favorite.

I loved you the most.

Really.

Jake opened his eyes, sighed. He blinked and rubbed his forehead. Staring up at the moonlit rafters of the house, his father's dream lingered in his mind. He reached under the blanket, under the hem of his designer boxers, and scratched his balls. He brought his fingers to his nose and smelled, eyes closed. He sniffed again.

"Fuck!" He lurched out of bed and stomped down the stairs into the main room. One of the computers was still on from the video chat, its screen saver flickering blue and red in the dark. Jake fumbled in its dim light, feeling for the phone. His wrist snapped in a quick circle, dialing 0. Waiting, he held the phone to his ear and looked down at the computer. He hadn't yet noticed the words on the screen saver: *"Miracle" is the lazy man's name for hard work.*

"Yes, hello," Jake said, startled. "I need the sheriff's

department." He felt behind him in the dark and settled into the chair. "Yes, I need to speak to the sheriff, please. Yes, him. Tell him it's Jake Barnes calling. Yes, his son."

Jake leaned back in the chair. His free hand traveled down to his crotch and rubbed the tent in his boxers.

"There's something going on out here I think you might want to investigate."

"Well, Sheriff, I think that's so sweet of you to help out poor Jake Jr. here."

Across the room, Jake winced. *Not "Junior." Please, anything but that.* The sheriff looked over at him and winked.

"Well, we haven't had much excitement around here lately, anyway," the sheriff said, turning back to the minister's wife. He handed her a sheaf of papers and pamphlets. "I found these in with the dry goods. They're for the Betamax."

"Thank you," she said, taking the papers. "Let's see now, we put that by the quadraphonic over there I believe." She surveyed the kitchen, now full of women tending to boxes, wadding newspaper, sorting disassembled equipment, tying up stacks of paper with twine, and stuffing them in zippered plastic baggies.

"How's the work going, Jake?" the sheriff said brightly, sauntering into the living room. "No more bears getting in your way?" The sheriff looked back over his shoulder at the women, grinning merrily. "Did you hear about Jake's bear attack last night?"

The women chuckled and shook their heads. "Sheriff, don't tease the poor boy," the minister's wife scolded. "He is from *Hollywood* after all. Jake ignore, him! A possum could scare anyone who hadn't seen one before."

The sheriff and Jake stood close, separate from the women in the kitchen.

"It sure felt like a bear," Jake murmured under his breath. "Grrr…"

The sheriff grinned. "Barely made it out the back door when they all showed up," he whispered. "Felt like some cheatin' husband."

"They sure showed up early enough."

"Your father checking out so close to the First Presbyterian annual bazaar, and leaving all his stuff for you to do with as you please—that's clearly the hand of God in motion."

"Clearly." Jake nodded over at the women. "They were just dying with curiosity when they got here. Who knows what they imagined was inside this place. But I think they've been pretty disappointed. We've packed up all these boxes of clothes. Coveralls and work shirts and jeans and boots and plain white socks. T-shirts, underwear. All the same mail-order shit he got us when we were kids. Quell boring. I told them they could just take it for themselves, but I don't think any of them liked the idea of their sons and husbands wearing my dad's underwear. Same with all the kitchen stuff and tools. None of them wants to eat after him. It's all going to the bazaar. The electronics, though—that's another story."

"Yeah, everybody knew Jake had tons of toys—everyone saw him picking up deliveries at the post office."

"Their husbands want it, but she told me she wouldn't let any of them come and get in her way. It's all going to be at the bazaar."

"Quite an assembly line she's got going."

"I think she's pretending she's working for Sotheby's. We've been at it all day. Matching instructions with warranties and receipts and cables and adapters and equipment. Taking apart the equipment, that's my job." He raised an eyebrow, "Since I'm the *man* here."

The sheriff nodded knowingly. "Has she mentioned her daughter yet?"

"We're supposed to have dinner."

"We'll have to find some business to take you away from that."

"Business would be good."

"All the house paperwork and taxes and such? Lawyer probably needs to have you go over those again, doesn't he?"

"Funny how that lawyer only works nights, hmm?"

"People do funny things in small towns."

"I ain't complaining about how you do things."

"Then I'll have to try something different tonight."

"Sheriff?" came a call from the kitchen. "You think you could take some of these boxes over to the church on your way back into town?"

Jake smiled and made a "call me" gesture, his outstretched thumb and pinky near his ear. The sheriff chuckled at him and nodded. "Sure thing. I'm heading out now," he called back into the kitchen.

The afternoon light filled the loft with yellow haze. Jake sat on the floor, leaning against the open steamer trunk, pouring through its hoard scattered on the floor around him.

"Instruction book," he sighed, placing a thin white pamphlet onto a stack of similar booklets. He picked up a green paperback textbook with torn corners. "Hey!" he said. "¡Hola!" He looked at the back cover, reading aloud. "'¿Donde esta Juanita?' '¿Por que esta Carlos triste?'" Jake shook his head. *¿Por que es la homeschooling muy shitty educación para los niños?*

He tossed the book through the air trying to land it in a large cardboard box labeled Trash. It hit the side and bounced off, scattering papers tucked inside onto the floor.

"Faggot muy grande!" Jake stood up, clasped his hands above his head, as if accepting the applause of a roaring crowd. He walked over to the papers, picked them up, held them over the trash box, and froze.

Gravesend First Congregational Newsletter.

Jake turned over the flyer, eyes falling to a portrait of a smiling woman in the lower right-hand corner. Her long blonde hair was ironed straight and cascaded smoothly over her ears. A thin gold locket dangled over the front of her dark blouse, which was buttoned up to the neck. No discernible makeup. Almost Jake's age. Head tilted in an inquisitive, submissive manner, but something fierce fired from her dark brown eyes. Her smile was set too certainly. Her white, white teeth clenched too hard.

The caption read, *Ashleys Celebrate Daughter's Return.* Jake scanned the article.

Mr. and Mrs. John Ashley are happy to announce the return of their daughter, Miss Brett Alicia Ashley, to Gravesend. For the past two years, Miss Ashley has been staying with friends of the family in exotic Siam, where Mr. Ashley has business interests. The Ashleys will be holding a wintertime ball to celebrate their daughter's return next Thursday, December 12. The Ashleys' celebrations are always the place to be, and this affair is certain to be one of their most outstanding efforts. It will also be an opportunity to hear finally the tales of Miss Ashley's exotic Siamese adventures!

The minister's wife called up the stairs, "You find anything more up there, Jake?"

"Yeah," Jake said, voice unsteady. "Just some, uh, legal stuff." He walked over to the edge of the loft and called down. "I'm going to have to go into town. I need to make copies of this for my brothers."

Jake looked over his shoulder at the snapshot on the wall of the four of them. "We've already packed up the scanner, haven't we?" he asked.

"That big flat thing? Yes, that's gone."

Copy shop probably has one, Jake thought. He went over and took the picture off the wall.

Jake hunched over the computer tucked in the copy shop's corner window. He paid no attention to the settlers of Oregon City passing by outside, peeking in at the stranger with the shaved head.

Set beside him were two flat envelopes, one with an Alaskan address, one destined for Brooklyn. Onscreen his email was addressed to his brothers in New York and Dallas, and cc'd to his home account. The attachment window listed two files: "Brett" and "Us."

We have to go to Gravesend, he typed.

"Well, look who wandered into town." The sheriff waved; the door jangled shut behind him.

Jake looked up, startled, and minimized the window of his email. "Hey."

"Hey yourself. Bears scare you out of the house?" He grinned.

Jake swallowed. "No, I—we'd already packed up the computers there. No bears."

"Maybe I should come out to make sure," the sheriff said, voice lowering.

"I had to make copies," Jake said. "Of some things I found." He handed the sheriff a set of copies. His eyes narrowed, looking them over.

"This is the lady that's supposed to be mother of one

of you?"

Jake nodded.

The sheriff frowned. "Jake, look at this other picture. How could you all not be brothers?"

"You know," Jake whispered. "Some things about Dad — they don't make natural sense. Dad could — do things. You know. Like that murder he solved for you."

"Yeah, that." He ran his tongue along his front teeth.

"We're going to have to meet her. We're all going to go back east where she lives."

"I thought you might stick around here a while longer." The sheriff folded his arms across his chest. "I thought we were — getting to know each other." He looked over at the copy shop counter; the woman who ran the store was busy in the back wrapping a large package.

"Jake," he said. "Do you know what you're really doing?"

"It's hard to know what's real in my family. It looks now like Dad might be right. Somehow, some way, one of us may not be real. May not be a real brother. I've got to find out who it is, to find out if it's me."

"You're real, Jake. You're real enough for me. And I think you and I might be on to something real."

Jake sat back down at the computer. "I have to do this," he said, staring at the screen. "I have work to do. I thought you of all people here would understand that." He looked pointedly at him.

The sheriff nodded slowly, eyes cloudy. He carefully and precisely folded the copies into quarters and slid them into the tight chest pocket of his uniform shirt.

"Well, Jake," he said quietly, "I do. I don't want you to go, but I do understand." He put his hand on Jake's shoulder. "And I'll be here for you when you're done." He turned on his heels and walked out of the shop.

Jake scowled, face red and eyes wet. He opened the email window again. *I found these going through Dad's stuff upstairs. We all have to go to Gravesend...*

TEXAS

A fly fixedly sipped sweat beads off Jake's forehead. With a wheezy exhale, Jake unsettled it. The insect reeled around the cab of the pickup, jerking and darting in the air. It resettled on the back of Jake's sticky neck, creeping close to the uniform red bristles rising up his nape. Asleep, Jake's eyes danced under their lids.

The rest stop had been empty when he'd pulled in for a nap. Jake had left his windows rolled down, hoping to catch what desiccated drafts might meander his way. The stress of expressway traffic, his girlfriend's anxiety about his leaving, and his own, secret dread over this familial undertaking had gnawed his nerves all day. And his father was still dead, although he couldn't quite believe it.

When stressed, Jake slept. Naps crept up his shirtsleeves, shimmied the back of his neck, swirled around inside his mouth. They pounced into his brain like a playful yet insistent house cat: "Sleeeep...now now NOW!" Druggy and seductive as morning sex, Jake could rarely say no. He'd learned to concoct multiple errands during crunch times at the garage to slip away for naps. Whenever he crashed out on the couch right after work, his girlfriend knew something was bothering him.

Giggles. Jake blinked at the sunlight. He ran his hand across his slick face. More giggles. Squinting, he turned to his right.

Two towheaded kids, peering in the passenger-side window of the cab, burst into hysterics.

"Caitlin! Cody! You two leave that man alone!"

62

ONE OF THESE THINGS IS NOT LIKE THE OTHER

Jake jumped, the shout shattering the lingering happy aura of the dream in which he'd been immersed. The kids scampered across the parking lot, yelling. The mother shot Jake an unmistakable glare: touch my children, and I'll kill you.

Jake blinked and pushed out his lower lip, turning away from the unpleasant lady. He tried to revive his interrupted dream. He closed his eyes and screwed up his face in concentration. No specifics came, only a warmth around his arms, chest, and heart. *I was dreaming about Mom again.*

Jake opened his eyes. He turned on the truck's ignition. He checked his satellite-positioning device, punched in the 8-track, and cranked the volume. He left the rest stop for the town where he was born.

Don't know what to believe anymore. Guess that's why I'm here. It's not just what the rest of us are thinking—if one of us is fake.

What pisses me off <u>most</u> is that I'm even thinking about all this. It's just gotta be more of Dad's bullshit. His final, ultimate fucking with us. CRAZY, that's all it is—and that's <u>not</u> what I am.

I can't stand he still has power to make me even halfway consider it, think about it, chase my tail like I am down here to New Garton just to try to prove him wrong. Or prove him right? Deep down, I wonder what I really want to be real. I don't know. Just <u>pisses the hell</u> out of me I can't brush it all aside, say fuck the old goat and forget about it.

I do know some things for sure. I know I had a mother. I've always known that. Is she the woman buried out back of our old cabin, here in New Garton somewhere? Here where we were born. Where he <u>said</u> we were born.

What if I'm not from here? What if I'm from Brooklyn? I remember having a mother. None of the rest of us do. My memories of her feel weird, they feel—Indie. Maybe I'm fake. Maybe that's why I'm here—so I can find out before they do.

If this Brett Ashley really is connected to us, to one of us, if one of us is really fake, how many other lies did Dad tell? How many secrets did he have?

Could one of us have really been born in Brooklyn? Could I really be a <u>New Yorker</u>?

He always said the name of this town clear as day, complaining about all the snoopy folk. "Small towns are just as sick as cities." He always said New Garton was our birthplace, and we believed him. There aren't any birth certificates to prove him wrong. None of us ever came back to this place—until me, until now. None of us ever tried to come home.

I want to find out much as I can before any of us start heading up North. I want as much truth as I can get before any of us meet this Brett Ashley woman.

If it's me—if I'm one—I'll need all the truth I can get.

What if she looks just like Dad, and us? What if she doesn't?

WHY AM I EVEN THINKING ABOUT ALL THIS!!? JUST LOOK AT US—WE KNOW WHO WE ARE!

<u>I AM US!!</u>

Jake slammed down his pen. He slapped shut the leather cover of his journal. He flushed, guilty over treating rough the present from his girlfriend.

There was a presence behind him. Turning to peer over the back of the booth, he met the gaze of a waitress reading over his shoulder. Face fixed, she didn't look away, just casually swept back her strawish hair, tucking the jaw-length bob behind her ear. Gray streaked the blonde; her eyes remembered blue. Crowsfeet and minimal makeup, she was middle-aged and appeared disinterested in disguising it. Her starched, yellow uniform fit well.

"Writer, huh," she stated more than asked. She held a coffeepot close to her bosom, withholding the java as if in ransom for a reply.

Jake glanced at his empty cup.

"Sure," he said. "Sure thing, yes, ma'am."

"You another damn journalist?" Her suspicious eyes drilled him, peering as she clutched the coffeepot closer.

"Oh, no, ma'am!" he reassured her. "This is just for me. It's private, not news stories. It's just, ah, my family tree."

"Really now?" Her countenance unclouded. "Well, hell, that's different." She leaned close to Jake and filled his cup to the brim. "I think it's nice when people take care to look up their family roots."

"Yes, ma'am." Jake smiled and grabbed one packet of sugar, two of nondairy creamer.

"Don't worry, kid." She straightened up and smiled. "I was afraid you were another damn reporter. They been all over this town like flies on shit last few weeks. Bloodsuckers all hoping for another Waco."

"Excuse me?" Jake said, shaking his packet.

"You know, all those people the FBI burned up? Remember? That cult over in Waco? Looked for a while like we might have the same thing here with those Illuminateds."

"Beg pardon? The Illuminateds?" Stirring, Jake clanked his spoon against the ceramic mug.

The waitress slid into the seat across from him. "Don't you watch the news or nothing?"

Jake shrugged and took an experimental sip. He nodded, blew on the coffee to cool it, and sipped again.

"Oh, kid, you missed a good show." She whistled and shook her head. "I've lived here most my life, and that foolishness beat all. See, we had these folks from Hong Kong? They come move here about five years ago. Part of some crazy cult from over there. You know why they picked New Garton to come to? 'Cause they saw it on a map and thought 'Gar-ton' meant 'God-town.' 'New God Town'! They thought *this* shithole was *Heaven*."

She gestured out the coffee shop window, indicating the forlorn motel with its parking lot empty save Jake's truck. She stroked her neck thoughtfully.

"They all lived together in this big, communal ranch house. They were real quiet and polite, but you should've seen them! They all wore these big white terry cloth, bathrobe things. Looked like they all just stepped out of the shower. After they'd been here a few months, they all started wearing big white cowboy hats, too. Bunch of Chinese folks all running around in white cowboy hats and fuzzy muumuus. No one paid them much mind, except for a laugh. Never even knew for sure how many of them were out there. But they never gave no one any trouble.

"Out of the blue last spring they sent this press release all over Texas, to damn near every newspaper, radio, and TV station. Turns out up inside that ranch of theirs they had computers and ditto machines and ham radios, all sorts of things. Their head pooh-bah, he sends out this big announcement saying that God done told him he's going to appear on TV. God's going to do a little show on Channel 13, June 15th, 1:15 p.m. We all just laughed, but then the reporters showed up. From Dallas, Austin, San Antone—they came from all over, and they flew in all these Yankee professors with them. Started saying all how these people could get really *cranky* if they get stood up by God. Space cowboys might all kill themselves! Crazy cults. You know some bunch in Tokyo once tried to kill everyone on the subway with poison gas?"

Jake shook his head and sipped his coffee.

"Well, they did. You watch out for Asian cults, now. America might have serial killers, but those Asian cults are a trip." She nodded decisively.

"So the big day comes, and they've been all getting ready, baptizing each other down in Hermann Creek, getting mud and crawdads all over their nice white robes. Reporters were crawling all around their ranch getting stuck on the barbed wire, watching Channel 13 on their little wristwatch TVs. And of course, nothing happens. So everyone gets all nervous for about an hour 'til they all come out of the house, singing! Their leader guy says, Oops! He was wrong, it's gonna be *next* week. And this time God's not gonna be on TV, he's gonna show up right at the ranch, live and in person."

She raised her eyebrows and rapped the table right in front of Jake.

"So we go through the whole damn thing again. Reporters get all worked up, nothing happens, then they all come out of the ranch, smiling ear to ear. You know what he says then?"

Looking over his coffee cup, Jake raised his eyebrows.

"Their big man gets up there and says, 'God is here now. *We* are God!'"

She leaned back in the booth, shaking her head. "'*We* are God!' Sounded like some therapy group." She clicked her tongue. "People parading their foolishness about for everyone to see, and the media just gobbling it up. Now foolishness is all people think about Texas. Used to be it was dead presidents, cowboy movies, that TV show. Now it's all Waco and these crazy Illuminateds, that murdering cheerleader mom, that farmer that kept a heifer in his bedroom."

She shook her head, smoothed her blouse. "But you, now," she said. "You're a good kid. Just looking up your family, hmm?" She refilled his coffee.

Jake nodded.

"So you're from around here?" She touched his hand.

Jake shrugged, scratching his crewcut. "I don't think we have any relatives still here. We're a real small family. Just my brothers and me, and our dad, and—he said our mom, she died in childbirth."

"Oh, that's a shame. Terrible shame."

"Well, yes, ma'am, except—" Jake frowned. "We don't know much about her. I'm here hoping to find some answers, since this is where we were born, my brothers and me."

"So you're hometown boys! How long you been gone? Must've left before you were football age, or I would've remembered you."

Jake stroked his mustache. "Yes'm, we left right after we were born. I'm fixing to go over to the courthouse today and look through the birth records."

"How old are you?"

"Twenty-four," Jake replied.

She shook her head. "Courthouse only has birth records from the last seventeen years. When they did their big switch-over to computers, just at the last minute, the fella in charge ended up erasing everything before that. And—" she paused, arching her eyebrows, "the fool had already cleaned out the originals. Can you beat that? Idiot."

She pursed her lips in concentration. "You might try over at the clinic. Or you been out to the cemetery? What's your mom's name, anyway?"

Jake looked at his diary, stroking its smooth cover. "I'm not sure exactly, I think—"

"Don't know your momma's name? Were you boys adopted?"

Jake shook his head. "No, our father just—never told us much about her. He just died."

The waitress smoothed her apron, searching for appropriate words. "Not to speak ill of the recently passed," she said with a deferential nod, "but a father should tell his boys all about their momma."

"I couldn't agree with you more."

"I was fixing to say, there used to be an orphanage over in Esperanza, but y'all wouldn't've been there if y'all still had your daddy. Hmm. Well, don't think I can offer much help, but I am sorry to hear about your loss."

Jake nodded. "So you don't maybe remember anything from back then?"

"Oh, kiddo, that was a long time ago—"

"But it would've been on the news and everything. There were four of us boys. Quadruplets."

"Four?"

"That only happens one in eleven million births," he added proudly.

Her eyes narrowed. Her lips pulled pale, tight.

Jake leaned forward. "Are you all right?"

She hastily extracted herself from the booth, crashing his water glass to the floor in the process.

The cook scurried out from the kitchen. "Hey, you okay?" He looked warily at Jake.

"Yeah, yeah." She drew her hand to her chest, fingers curling into a fist, and jerked her head toward Jake. "This man here needs to pay up his bill and leave. I've got to clean myself up." She plucked her notepad from her apron pocket, ripped off a sheet, and slapped it on Jake's table, avoiding his eye.

The cook watched her hurried retreat into the kitchen. An unseen door slammed and the men faced each other. The cook stepped forward.

"What did—" Jake said.

"Don't worry," the cook said. He broke into a lingering smile, fixing his gaze on Jake. "Don't worry about her. Let me get this." Stepping closer, he bent to pick up the larger chunks of glass.

"You staying over at the motel?" he asked Jake. He looked up at him, face almost grazing Jake's knee, palm cupping glass shards.

Jake pulled his legs together. Glaring at the cook, he grabbed the check from the table and stepped back.

The cook carried the shards back behind the counter, appraising Jake as he dropped them in the trash.

ONE OF THESE THINGS IS NOT LIKE THE OTHER

Jake scowled at the bill, which lacked a total. He threw a twenty down on the table and stormed toward the door.

"Hey, bro—" the cook called out.

"Keep the change," Jake barked. He whipped out the keys to his pickup.

Jake sat cross-legged in the center of the bed. He'd stripped the bedspread. His girlfriend had said motels never washed them. She'd told him how she'd seen a consumer investigator use a blue light to illuminate hidden piss, blood, cum. Jake eyed the impotent heap of bedspread in the corner. *It'd be like sleeping with all the people who have been here before me.*

Jake cradled the phone between his legs. Around himself he'd arranged a semicircle of foldout driving maps: New Garton, West Texas, Texas, the Southwest, the United States, North America. He bought fresh maps whenever he went on a trip. Sometimes he replaced them before the trip was over. Jake did not write on the maps. He did not underline destinations or circle routes. He feared obscuring crucial information, but, mostly, he loved them too much. He loved their precision, their thoroughness, their completeness. How they stood alone yet worked together. How an inset on one map was a whole world on another.

Jake used traditional foldout paper maps, but only until usage damaged their folds. Then he replaced them. Uneven folds and wrinkles marred their beauty. He kept some maps in tubes as if he were a ship's captain. They would uncurl for him, beautifully free of creases. Some he framed and mounted in the apartment.

Wish all maps were as nice as these. You can tell some work went into these. Wish the world was this proud and beautiful.

Jake didn't use compact, laminated maps. He didn't like their stingy coverage or incomplete keys and legends. The street he needed, never in their listings. Neighborhoods outside of the "area shown."

In college, he'd rented a house with three other kids in a poor neighborhood of northeast San Marcos. The city map had featured the publisher's seal smack-dab on top of his new address—as if no one in that neighborhood used maps, and no one who did use maps would be looking to go to that neighborhood. Exclusion from his hometown map had unsettled him.

The phone rang.

"Hi."

"Hey—it's me."

Jake smiled. "Hey, baby. How was class?"

She grunted. "I still think Elizabeth Bishop is a loca. How are things down there?"

"Not bad..." Jake traced a finger along the Rio Grande.

"You find what you're looking for?" Casual words, but her voice betrayed hesitancy, wariness.

"Aw, well. Guess I oughtta have a better idea what that is."

He could discern the shuffling sounds of his girlfriend sitting at the kitchen table, scooting her chair closer to the phone so the cord could reach.

"Well," she said, "did you find out anything? Were all four of you born there, together?"

"Don't know yet," Jake sighed. "They lost a whole bunch of records when they went to computers. Dad moved away right after we were born, so there shouldn't be any school records. I checked over at the newspaper, and there's no birth announcements, no wedding announcements, not even an article on quads, which should've been front-page news in a town like this."

"Maybe your old man was full of shit," his girlfriend suggested, her sarcastic quip followed by the click of her lighter and hiss of her inhale.

Jake faked a chuckle, knowing humor masked her concerns. "Aw, I guess we know that already."

"Yes. Eso es muy verdad," she said thoughtfully, then they both laughed, for real, at her gravity. "Oh, Jake. Maybe he never really lived there."

Jake nodded. "No, he lived here. Sheriff remembers him. I went to the police station this afternoon, after the paper."

"Really? What did he say?"

"She." Jake's pale skin reddened. He crinkled up his freckly nose and turned his eyes up to the ceiling. "It's a she. She's the sheriff. She doesn't remember Dad, but she remembers her dad talking about him. She's second-generation."

Pause. "¿Que?"

"Huh?"

"Second-generation what?"

"Oh! Sheriff." He looked back down, following grooves in the white-painted cinder blocks, settling on the dark TV's glass. He frowned. A paper pyramid on top advertised pay-per-view porn. Jake glanced at the adjacent bottle in a brown paper bag. He averted his eyes again and cleared his throat.

"Her dad was sheriff, too, for a long time. Dead now. But she said he used to tell her stories about crazy old Jake Barnes that lived out in the woods. She described him pretty well. I guess her dad would try to check up on Dad from time to time, make sure he didn't die out there, especially once he got married."

"Your mom?" Her voice sharpened.

"Well now, I don't know. Sheriff didn't know her name. Said she was real beautiful but wasn't a local girl. Everything seemed all right till—"

"Yeah?"

"She died. In childbirth, like Dad always said. Dad had tried to handle the delivery, but there were complications he couldn't handle, I guess. Sheriff had to have the body dug up. Dad had buried her behind the house, like he always said. Like I told you we always used to pretend."

"Like he had your brother do to him?"

"Yeah." Jake slid his tongue across his lips. "Medical examiner confirmed she died from natural causes, and that she'd just given birth, but no one saw the kids, or knows how many were born. Dad moved away right after. He kind of became even more of a bogeyman 'round here after that. Leaving town so quickly, what with his wife buried there and all." He leaned on the pillows stacked up against the cement. "Sheriff said she was pretty relieved to hear he was dead."

"That's not very nice."

"Aw, I didn't tell her who I was. She grew up hearing stories about him. No one here recognizes me, thank God. Must be the mustache and crewcut and all." He sat up straight. "I didn't plan on lying to her none. I just asked about Jake Barnes, and she started going to town. She went so far, it would've embarrassed her if I told her who I was."

His girlfriend exhaled. "Relax, baby."

Jake pursed his lips, mustache bristling. "I told her I

worked with the bank handling his estate, that we were trying to track any family he might have."

"Ah. And no one knows?"

"Yeah."

Jake rolled over, curling on his side into the pillows. He began to stretch his legs, but looked warily at the maps around him and drew himself into his chest.

"Well, Jake, it sounds terminado," she said. "You coming back home now?"

"No, I'm sorry, hon, not yet. There's something—"

"What? Why not?"

Jake braced himself, knowing she wouldn't like hearing this. "When I first got here, I was talking to this waitress. Older gal, local, real friendly. Thought it was real sweet I was looking up my family tree."

"She don't know much."

"She was real sweet back at me till I started talking about quads. Then she got all upset and left." He breathed slowly, listening for her reaction. "I need to check things out here a little bit more. I struck some kind of nerve with her. Something about us. I've got to stay and try to find out what she knows."

His girlfriend sighed, her respiration offering up no subtleties that Jake could suss out. "Hon," she said firmly, "I'm worried. I want you to make peace with your family, but I am afraid. And I know you are, too."

"What do you mean?"

"You were having dreams again before you left."

Jake shook his head. "Hon—" he protested, but she continued.

"It just doesn't feel good: Your dad, who we know was crazy, tells you more crazy stories before he kills himself. You all harassed this poor woman out east, who your father probably just pulled out of a phone book. He's got you all thinking that one of you is some kind of imposter, when all you have to do is look at each other to see how ridiculous that is. Just look at each other. Look at yourselves. You're all thinking you're going to go see this woman, who doesn't even want to see you guys, so first you got to go off alone back to where you were born. Thinking you're some private detective, going looking around, turning over rocks—"

"All I'm doing is looking for the truth. For some answers,

is all," he said, letting his anger show. "A man's got to do that sometimes."

She let him listen to silence. He eyed the bottle. "You better take care of yourself, Jake Barnes," she muttered. "When you go turning over rocks, sometimes you find all sorts of nasty vermin under there."

"Don't worry," he said, correcting his tone. "Hon, I'll be careful. I love you, you know."

"Yes, I love you, too. Okay. Well. Hurry back. Soon."

"Call you tomorrow?"

"Sure. Sleep well."

"You too. Buenas noches."

"Buenas noches."

Jake hung up, stood up, circled around the room a few times. He pulled the tequila from its brown, noisy bag and set the bottle of sloshing gold on his nightstand. He got his guitar case from the closet and laid it on the bed. He turned the adult-movie sign facedown.

I know you.

I know the nap of sand in the nook of your eye in the morning. I know the seemingly infinite difference of your freckles: the cardinals, nutmegs, and inks strewn across your person intercomparable to an invading infantry, occasioning your skin to consider itself foreign. I know how inhales tickle under your nose. How running your tongue along that zone initiates enjoyable sensations. I know the tender, unusual nubs inside your ear canal, unseen miniature enigmas. Silken like earwax, enticing to scrape, but years of bloody nails negated that notion. I know your feet never encounter shoes extensive enough; the pinky toe on one foot nudges its neighbor, nail hunched at a twenty-nine-degree angle. Another pinky bends under its neighbor, as if to hide in the foot. I know your tongue's annoying foundation 'n' the nectar high in your throat's pinnacle. I know the one incisor, so needlelike your tongue continually nuzzles it. You nosh pencils to note the deep, enjoyable indentations in the wood.

You wound your knuckles with wales and calluses, but not from work. To wit, you go wacko with nails, wambly with their feel. Why, you cut them with frequency; you're wholly calm only when each is trimmed and filed to the tip. You hate knowing them. Worry-ridden, you wildly wedge whatever visible nail-edge has worked its way out into nearby flesh. Pinky-nail wedges into knuckle on ring finger;

ring-finger nail wedges against knuckle of fuck finger, which wedges against index, which wedges back against fuck finger. All wedge against thumb ball. No wonder each of your pressure spots is wonderfully alpenglow, wantonly wounded, warped and worn by you.

You're unable to enucleate the neurotic urge. Why don't you just keep an ultrafine file near you unceasingly, so the ubiquitous edges never unfurl? You ultimately cut and file them once or twice a week, but it's still not pure, unadulterated satisfaction. Your ultimatum remains being caught in an intersection of ultramundane obsession and unavailing indolence.

Your dream, the only denouement you can understand, is a metal glove or brace, which would divide your fingers, distant and disassociated in order to disable crowding them against each other. You couldn't yield to the desire to produce pressure toward your fingernail edges. Your hand would be in a determined and steady widespread attitude, as if enduringly enumerating to 'five.'

I understand the hurried hurt that hotly holds your asshole after hours, arousing you from shut-eye, or hampering your return to shut-eye after a wholesome shit. The hard ache heavy within. You've never told your doctor or girlfriend because they'll suspect you achieved it via having your behind cornholed. I know how happy those ice cubes make you feel when held around your behind half an inch from the hole, held against that nether space halfway between your hole and hairy huevos. I know how that ice is hot and yet is the only thing that helps the horrible hurt.

Then your whole physique is covered with the hideousness of that translucent, thin top layer of parchmenty epithelium, stretched too tight over amethyst and indigo veins, and dotted with Castilian red. The silly amaranth tone of your crotch hair. You witness it while having that morning hard-on discharge and think hastily that someone played a practical jest on you, shaded that body hair while you slept, then you remember — and following all these lengthy years it nevertheless takes that thoughtful flash to think — this is natural. This is who I am.

I am you; I know these things. I am that you are. I am so that you can be. And I must be for you to be.

Jake opened his eyes, sniffed. He swung his legs over into the side of the motel bed. He blinked and tugged his mustache, his father's dream lingering in his mind.

"Guess it's about time for breakfast anyway," he said wearily.

ONE OF THESE THINGS IS NOT LIKE THE OTHER

Jake returned to the coffee shop. Today was Sunday. Churchgoing clusters just released from early service filled the booths, chattering away in short-sleeve dress shirts and doily-collar dresses. Jake smelled bacon and sausage, sweet maple and eggs with hot sauce. It was a happy place. He was glad to be there and wished he could linger, wished he had no plan, no agenda. He placed himself on a counter stool, its round seat sporting torn orange vinyl. Jake swiveled around and squinted at the Sunday morning light, beyond bright already at eleven, soon to give way to afternoon's relentless glare. Outside, across a wide bank of burnt grass, massive trucks barreled down the highway. A yawn gripped Jake and he covered his mouth, catching with his breath a last taste of his father's dream.

The waitress bustled over to him, flipping her notepad. "Now what can I get you this morning?" She looked up. Her smile vanished.

Jake forced innocent cheer. "Hometown Combo, please."

Eminently unimpressed, she merely said, "Eggs?"

"Scrambled, dry."

"Hash browns? Grits?"

"You got cheese grits?"

She raised an eyebrow. "Of course."

"That'll do me fine."

"Pancakes?"

"Yes, please."

"Compote?"

"Peach."

"Mm-hmm." She shot his coffee a perfunctory glance and spun around. Returning behind the counter, she ripped his order from her pad, clipped it to the kitchen's chrome carousel. "Hometown!" she called out to the cook.

Breakfast unfolded neatly like a new map. She brought Jake his meal and tended to other customers. He did not attempt to charm her with chitchat or sweet talk. She kept his coffee full, punctually set down his check and returned change. She avoided his eye. He said, "Thank you kindly, ma'am." The tip: generous, not showy.

"Quadruplets have never been born in this town." The clinic's office attendant spoke flatly, glaring at Jake from the other side of a sliding window. "I have seen this town's every medical record from the last fifty years. I supervised our computer transfer."

Jake pushed out his cheek with his tongue, pursed his lips, contemplating the brittle man before him. He nodded. "You handle the courthouse records, too?"

The attendant narrowed his eyes at Jake. "I am also the genealogical officer for the county Historical Society. I would certainly know about anything so—freakish."

Jake's left knee twitched. Tight at his side, he clenched his fists into small balls, rough-chewed nubs of nails pressing into sweaty flesh.

As if swatting flies, the attendant waved away the air in front of him. "So. I don't know what else I can say to convince you. Did you talk to anyone over at the *Progress*?"

"Yeah. There's no quads in the birth announcements from that year. Or the year before. Or after."

"Probably because there were none born here then. Or ever." He leaned into the window, propping his elbows on the counter and resting his chin on his hands. He blinked at Jake. "Maybe you're not really from here. Did you consider that option? We're the only clinic. That's the only paper. Maybe you got your towns mixed up. I believe you said you moved away when you were very young? Perhaps this is not your home."

Jake pushed away from the window. He stormed through the waiting room, dodging the knees of a large woman in a plastic school chair. He bumped the children's table and sent a stack of colored plastic blocks tumbling. Ignoring them, Jake yanked open the door and, despite being blinded by the long orange arms of the evening sun, threw himself down the cement steps into the parking lot. He stood there and defiantly lit a cigarette. Sucking it greedily, he leaned against the County Clinic sign.

Behind him, the front door creaked open. Jake looked over his shoulder to see the woman from the waiting room peek out. She smiled at Jake. She stepped through the door, easing it shut behind her. She tiptoed down the steps, lifting her embroidered denim poncho off the ground. The lenses of her wide, round glasses blackened in the sun.

"Thought you might still be out here," she cooed, fidgeting with the bulky shell necklace at her throat. She sidled up beside him and nodded at his smoke. "Got one of those for your mama, now?"

"What?"

"Relax, child, relax. I'm old enough to be your mama, aren't I, hmm?" She patted her bun of rusty gray hair. "But I'm not. I just meant friendly mama, like Mama Cass. I already got one kid, and he's all the trouble I can afford. He's adopted, too."

Jake nodded, handing her a smoke. "I can't have no kids," she said, then added in a dramatic whisper, "female trouble."

She held out her palm, stopping any show of sympathy. "It was my saving grace; kept me from having too many babies when I was your age and sleeping around all over Texas."

She laughed. He lit her cigarette. She inhaled happily. "He's inside with the doctor now, so I thought I'd sneak out here and check on you. This is a hard town for strangers."

"I thought I might not be one."

"So I heard." She smiled. "Sorry for eavesdropping, child, but you know this *is* a small town. We've got to do what we can to keep ourselves entertained. Our paper don't have a Business section. It's got a None-of-Your-Business section!"

She smiled merrily at her joke then silenced, cocking her head at Jake's shirt. In a quick, fluid motion at once motherly and punctilious, she whipped out Jake's chest-pocket flap, buttoned and smoothed it.

"Thank you," he said. "So, how long you lived here? You ever hear anything about quadruplets being born?"

She took a drag and nodded, leaning against the sign beside him. "No." She exhaled shook her head. She held the lipstick-smudged filter before her sunglasses for inspection. "I was born here," she said, "but I spent my younger days gallivanting all over the country. Didn't come back to New Garton regular until about ten years ago."

She pursed her lips. "But there are people I've known here since I was born. I know a *whole* lot of dirt. F'rinstance, I know there's other kinds of birth information in this town. Place to go looking for babies that you probably haven't checked. Babies that didn't get written down anywhere. Children that escaped record-keeping."

Jake stood up straight and turned to face her. "What are you talking about?"

She smiled. "Back years ago," she said, "we had here some

folks doing things the natural way."

Jake shielded his eyes against the rays of the evening sun. They gilded him head-to-toe so that his carroty hair no longer stood out anomalous but blended into a unified whole, a solid orange gold man of unified hue.

"Midwifery," she said. "Some local kids, when they came back from college, they set up sort of a secret clinic here. Herbal abortions and natural births. Snuck babies to the orphanage over in Esperanza. Helped all the ding-dong hippie girls, Junior Leaguers who hid secrets for months under baggy sweaters. It was two folks, a couple. The man, he'd been a med student. Everyone in town had high hopes—our first homegrown doctor. I think he'd made it to interning before he decided instead to go 'change the system.'" She cackled.

"No kid they birthed was ever announced in the paper or anything. People just kept quiet about it. Most of them weren't from around here. And those that were, well, once the babies were here, they were so sweet no one had the heart to press charges. They had a friend at the courthouse who handled the birth certificates. Lots of secrets in small towns." She smiled proudly.

"Are they still here?"

She tossed her butt across the lot. "Well, he's not. Polio took him down. Very strange, so late in life. Kinda funny, his almost being a doctor and all. But even a doctor can't do nothing about something like that."

She lowered her eyes, voice quieting. "She wanted to take care of him, but when it came time for the iron lung—" She trailed off, shaking her head. Jake watched her intently, but the sunset darkened her into nothing but a silhouette. "He went away," she said. "So did she. She came back."

"The woman—the midwife?"

"Mm-hmm." She looked back up, adjusting her poncho. "This gal'd know about all sorts of babies that slipped through the cracks." She covered her mouth and giggled. "'Slipped through the cracks'! Get it? Oh!" She composed herself. "Ole Pissy inside knows all about her, but pretends none of it ever happened. Wants to keep the town's history pure."

Jake's breath quickened. "What's she doing now?"

"She stopped doing all that after he died, of course."

Jake scratched his mustache. His eyes darted around the

parking lot. "Can you show me this lady?"

"Oh, you can't miss her, child. Sassy ole blonde. Well, what's left of a blonde. Works over at the coffee shop. Just ask over there."

Jake nodded, swallowing.

"I gotta go check on my little monster," she said, skipping back up the steps. "Thanks for the ciggie-butt." She opened the door and peeked back out at Jake before returning into the clinic. "Good luck," she said.

"Hey mister!"

Jake stopped, startled. All week, whenever he'd come and gone from the motel, the strawberry blonde clerk had never noted his presence. She'd stared vacantly at the TV under her desk, occasionally munching bright orange snacks that painted her lips and fingers. Jake had never heard her speak.

"Got you a package."

"What?" Jake let the glass door close behind him, bell jangling, and walked over to the desk. She reached down to the floor beside her and set out a brown paper envelope on the counter. An abundance of clear tape wrapped the package in an excessive style Jake recognized.

"You're Jake Barnes, right?"

"Yeah."

"Well, here, then." She pushed the envelope across the counter. "It's from Dallas," she muttered, slouching into her usual position behind the counter.

Jake grabbed the package. It was from home. From his girlfriend.

"Thanks."

The clerk nodded, popping a snack into her mouth.

Jake walked over into the coffee shop. He eased up to a stool at the corner of the counter. He set the package on the orange laminate in front of him and sat. He eyed the package but did not open it, instead surveying the restaurant. Most of the before-work crowd had left. A few seniors lingered, a noisy tourist family, and a pair of women in supermarket vests. Jake eyed them all discreetly. No one seemed to be stealing glances at the stranger who was becoming a repeat customer. He'd been there the evening prior, but the former-midwife waitress hadn't been working. He hadn't asked after her. Today, she was on the job.

He calmly placed his order; she took it with indifference, then returned to her tasks: polishing glassware, placing ketchup bottles mouth-to-mouth to consolidate contents, arranging parallel the plastic-wrapped pie slices in the rotating dessert tower.

Finally Jake picked up the package, turning it over in his hands. Clear sealing tape encased almost the entire envelope. Mummified it.

Jake grabbed his butter knife. He stabbed the blade in a corner and sawed open a side. The dull serration stretched rather than sliced the tape. Jake struggled to remove the casing, and he remembered skinning rabbits as a child.

Out fell a few pages of paper, a piece of cardboard for support. A small sheet of floral stationery was paper-clipped to the one page. *Jake,* his girlfriend's handwriting read, *these are from that email from your gay brother I told you about. This is scaring me. Come home soon.*

Jake detached her note and eyed his brother's message.

Sorry you haven't heard from me in a while. I've been busy working with all these women from the local church packing up Dad's stuff. They think they're working for Sotheby's or something. But I found these going through Dad's stuff upstairs. We all have to go to Gravesend...

Reading, he pushed pancake bits around a hot pool of cherry-pie filling.

"We want silver-dollar pancakes!" whined the tourist children in unison.

"They don't have silver-dollar pancakes," their parents repeated in a beleaguered monotone.

Jake looked up. The waitress flashed a stern glare as the tourist kids clambered from their booth. They pressed their faces against the glass souvenir case, ogling mints, gum, and wooden peg games. She watched them closely, poised to strike lest they disturb something they shouldn't.

Jake returned to the letter.

I made copies of the picture and the article for all

of you and that Ashley woman. She looks like quite the princess, doesn't she? We look like... Is that what we looked like? We certainly don't anymore. I don't know what we look like now.

I guess the article doesn't really give us much info. And it was the only thing about her I found. I can't tell why Dad would keep it. According to the article, it looks like she would've been in Siam when we were born. Dad never left the country, did he? Anyway, at least now we know what she looks like.

I've almost finished up here. Sorry it's taken so long. Let me know what you all are finding out. I'm not feeling you so much these days. We'll all be together soon. It's been a long time.

Hollywood hadn't signed the letter.

Jake held the picture of Brett Ashley and closed his eyes, taking slow, deep breaths. He pressed his lips together and set down the picture.

The waitress cleared Jake's plate without a word. Jake asked for a coffee refill. She hesitated before granting his request.

Jake smiled nervously. The cook rang a bell. "Order up!"

From the corner of his eye, Jake watched her walk past with plates of food. She rounded the corner and collided with a hiding tourist child. She gasped; the child screamed. Chilequiles splattered against the back of a booth, eggs and tortilla strips sliding down the orange vinyl. A whipped-cream-and-strawberry waffle slumped to the floor in a pink pile.

"My waffle!" whined the girl. She ran crying to her mother.

Jake jumped at his chance. He grabbed fistfuls of napkins and knelt on the floor beside her.

"Oh-oh, thank you," she muttered. He scooped ruined food onto plates and placed them on the counter. "No, you really don't—"

"Please, ma'am." He smiled apologetically. "Momma wouldn't like it if I just sat here and watched a lady clean up a mess like this."

She eyed him warily while retrieving scattered silverware.

She licked the inside of her cheek. "Well, thank you, son." She nodded and continued gathering the wreckage. "I'm glad to hear some folks still raise their children right." She turned her gaze pointedly from Jake to the tourist family, then looked back with a raised eyebrow. She and Jake exchanged grins.

"Why don't you go take care of them," Jake suggested. "I'll finish this. You got a rag behind the counter?"

She nodded. "Why, thank you. And there's some spray cleaner, too, back there." She smoothed her blouse, tucked hair behind her ear, and marched over to the distraught family.

When things settled, she returned to Jake. He was nursing a cold slosh of coffee dregs. She brought him the pot. He held his hand over the cup.

"No thanks, ma'am. I've got to go make a call."

"Oh? Well, then. Thank you for your help back there." She set down the pot and eyed him keenly. "You're Wild Jake's kid, right?"

"Yes, ma'am. Yes, I am."

"Thought so. I put it together after you were in here first time. Why you looked so familiar. He here with you?"

"No, ma'am. He just passed."

Her eyes widened. "Wild Jake passed?"

Jake nodded. She let out a long sigh. She looked down at her fingers.

"Well now," she whispered. "Well, well." She looked up abruptly. "I didn't mean no offense calling him that." Catching her breath, she sat down at the stool beside Jake.

"Don't worry, you're not the first person to call him that."

She nodded. "And what you said about your momma back there; I thought you said the other day your momma was dead."

Jake looked down, bashful. "Yes, well, I'm sorry about that. Saying she'd roll over in her grave just didn't seem very polite."

"I see what you mean. So both your folks are gone?"

He looked up at her. "We don't know for sure. That's why I'd appreciate if I could talk to you. There may be a lot we don't know. New things we're finding out. I think you might know some answers."

She reeled back her upper lip and ran her pink tongue across her front teeth. "You and your brothers?"

He nodded. Her eyes wandered along the counter to where the contents of Jake's package were spread out. She raised an eyebrow.

"Say," he said, "you ever hear of a place called Sotheby's?"

"Mm-hmm. They auction off rich people's crap." She wiped her hands on her apron and nodded at the tape-sealed envelope. "Who sent you that?"

"One of my brothers."

"He certainly likes his tape."

"No, that's my girlfriend. She forwarded it from him. She doesn't trust just a single piece of tape." Jake smiled. "She's the same way with Christmas presents. She'll start with little pieces of tape just to hold the paper folds in place. Then she'll seal each crease with a long strip. Then she'll run strips along every corner and package's edge — 'in case the paper rips.' Then she'll inspect the whole package, all worried. She'll run her finger along the leftover areas of exposed wrapping paper. Finally she'll sigh and start rolling the tape all along the gift, covering every inch until the whole package is covered up."

"That's not right, but it's sweet. Sounds like you miss her." She shook her head, smiling. She reached under the counter for a clean rag and set it in front of them both with a decisive air. "You gonna come in here every breakfast until I talk to you?"

"I'm almost as stubborn as my dad." Jake grinned.

She didn't smile, merely exhaled a short puff of air. "Okay, kiddo. But I get a dinner out of it."

"Sure thing, it'd be my pleasure."

"I'll meet you over in the lobby at eight — "

"I can pick you up — "

"No, you don't need to be coming around my house. I'll be at the motel lobby at eight, and you can take me to the steak house. And we can talk."

"All right. Eight o'clock. I'll be waiting."

She nodded and flicked her fingers absently toward the door. "All right, now scoot. Let me get back to work."

"Yes ma'am!" Jake left his money on the counter and backed out of the coffee shop.

Jake watched a scorpion scuttle across the phone booth's shelf. It was dark yellow and plump, like a golden raisin. The stinger, arched up over its back, quivered. With the back of his hand,

Jake flicked away the scorpion and squashed it under his boot.

Outside the phone booth, a dust storm was sweeping into town. Jake leaned against the booth's hot, cracked glass, which amplified the pings and snaps of sand and gravel bits hitting the booth. Through the thickening air, Jake could see horses drinking from the trough in front of the computer dealership, shaking their manes and snorting anxiously at the gusts of grit. The milk truck rattled past them, abandoning its route for now. Jacob kicked his boot impatiently against the side of the booth. Finally, his brother in New York clicked back on.

"Sorry about that," his brother said. "Reverse charges when we finish, okay? Or send me the bill. How much is this side trip costing you, anyway?"

"Don't worry about it. But there's a dust storm coming into town and—"

"Dust storm?" his brother laughed. "Tumbleweeds, too? Okay, I'll get to the point. Ah, let's see if I've got this all so far. The people you've been schmoozing down there remember Dad. So he wasn't entirely insane. We really are from New Garton. So, if one of us is some kind of clone, then New Garton is where the secret laboratory should be hidden."

"You don't have to be a smartass. Yeah, they remember him. And they say he was pretty crazy."

"Oh? Now, *that's* news. Is New Garton as awful as he used to say?"

"It's just Texas. Nothing special. Little bigger than most places we ever lived near. But it could've grown since then."

"Okay. Right. So Dad lived there. And he did have a wife, who died during childbirth."

"Right."

"Did he really bury her behind the house?"

"Yeah, that's part of why he became sort of a bogeyman after leaving."

Jacob laughed. "And according to what Holly found, he did know this Ashley woman. Or at least kept clippings about her. And that photograph of us. Dad's starting to look like George Washington here. With a sentimental streak. Yes, well. They don't know the half of it, do they? So what else?"

Jake sighed. "Our mother—his wife—whatever, the lady did die in childbirth. But they were doing it at home, so it happened there. And they were doing it on their own. No one was there with them, so no one knows for sure how many kids there were. There's no records. Dad'd come into town for supplies, but never let anyone near the house. He left town a few months later."

"So you haven't found anything that disproves what we've always known. Maybe he just ran into this Brett lady somewhere down the road," Jacob mused. "Maybe they had a fling, although that I can't imagine. Or maybe he just found that clipping somewhere and became obsessed with her. Who knows? So why are you still poking around down there?"

"Because!" Jake snapped defensively. "I've stumbled onto something. I didn't get anywhere with the medical records, but Jacob, listen: around the time we were born, here in New Garton there was this med-school dropout and his girlfriend. They used to run a sort of secret clinic here. Secret abortions and midwifing and stuff. We could've been part of this whole underground thing."

"The midwives or the abortions?"

Jake ignored his brother. "The med-school guy is gone, but there's this woman here. She's a waitress at a coffee shop. She was the midwife at this clinic. I met her. I just told her I was here to be looking up my family tree, and she was just real sweet. But when I told her we were quads, she got all bug-eyed and clammed up on me, like she knew something but didn't want to talk about it. Man, I think we *were* born here, and she knows something about it."

His brother digested this silently. Jake studied the shiny circles of the pay phone's dial: CRockett-6-7223 embossed across the reflection of his face.

"So are you going to talk to her again? Ask her if she knows this Brett Ashley person?"

"Yeah. This morning I finally got her to relax around me. I'm taking her out to dinner."

"You dog! Does your lovely girlfriend know about this?"

"Fuck off, she's old enough to be our mother."

"Maybe she is. Or maybe she's just yours. Kinky."

"Fuck you."

"You'll give me all the juicy details?"

"Look, are you still—"

"Yes, I've got my phone set on TRANSCRIBE. I'll fax carbons to the rest of us. Everyone will be up-to-date."

"Thanks."

"How much longer are you going to be down there?"

"Don't rightly know."

"Well, I talked to Holly out in Oregon. Apparently he's managed to convince our wilderness brother to leave the Alaskan tundra and come out here to New York. Imagine that. Can you get here in time to join them? We'll have a reunion," he added dryly.

"Yeah. I'll be there. We'll all be together."

"You aren't going to bring your girlfriend, are you?"

"No."

"Good. This is just for us. Band of brothers and all that. Don't drag anyone else into all the family madness just yet. And don't drag things out too long down there."

"I just reckon it'd be prudent to first get as many answers as we can, if we're gonna go busting in on this Ashley lady."

"I thought she was the one with all the answers."

"Aw, you heard how pissed she was on the phone! How you think she's gonna be with the four of us showing up on her doorstep like some long-lost scout troop? Maybe if we know some truth she'll trust us more. Or we'll know why she doesn't trust us."

Jacob sighed. "Yes, but we don't have forever to work on this. We've agreed on a time to meet. You can't be late."

"Aw, don't start with me like that—"

"Dal, do I need to remind you that I've got a life here? I'm in the middle of things. I've got things to do once we're done with all of this nonsense."

"Like what?"

"Well, there's this little hobby I've got about becoming a doctor." His brother paused. "And, once all of this family business is out of the way, I'm going to go ahead with converting. It requires a lot of preparation."

"What?"

"I'm going to go through with converting. To Judaism."

"You're really going to go ahead do that? Like being Jewish Born Again?"

"Yes, that's right," Jacob snapped. "'Jewish Born Again.'"

"And everyone's going to have to keeping calling you Jacob?"

"It's my name now."

"Whatever. Even if you convert, you still won't be a real Jew. I don't care if you cut up your dick or what."

"It's not an issue of 'realness.'"

"What does it mean if they'll let anyone convert? How special is it if anyone can join?"

"Dallas. I've already been through this. With all of us. It's what I'm doing. I just wanted to let you know my plate's a little bit on the full side, so, if you don't mind, I'd like to wrap up this little family reunion adventure ASAP."

"Fine. All right. Well, I won't dawdle around here. Wouldn't want finding out the truth of our family, our own mother for chrissakes, to get in the way of your precious Jew school."

"Dal—"

"Man, I'm really on to something here, okay? I'm really close to something, I can feel it."

"*What* can you feel?" his brother asked dubiously. "Why are *you* feeling so much all the sudden?"

Jake scraped his boot along the phone booth's wooden floor. "I can feel her," he said. "I can feel her, like we feel each other."

His brother said nothing.

"Ennie?"

"What do you mean 'feel' her? Our mother's dead. Or, like you seem to want to think, if this Brett woman *is* our mother, she's just over in Brooklyn, and I should be able to 'feel' her, and I can't 'feel' her. How could you 'feel' her all the way down in Texas?"

"I don't know. Maybe being back where we were born is bringing things back."

"Things?"

Jake pursed his lips. "I remember her."

"What?"

"I remember her. Mom."

"What do you mean, you remember her? We don't remember her. We've been trying all of our lives to remember her, and we've never been able to."

"I remember having a mom. I remember her holding me."

"You bastard. Where were the rest of us at this time? Huh? How the fuck come *we* don't remember this? You little shit. What are you trying to do?"

"What are you getting so pissed about? Look, this is real. I feel it."

"Fantasies always feel real. You're just getting worked up from this idea that one of us is an outsider. You want it to be you. You want to be all special and different with Brett. You want your mommy, your own mommy—you don't want to share her with anyone else."

Jake grunted, shook his head, and pressed his palm against the booth wall. "This isn't new. I've remembered this since—"

"What? Since when? What do you mean? How long have you had these special little memories all of your own?"

"I always have," Jake sighed. "I always have, and just lately it's been getting more powerful."

"Only you felt this, none of the rest of us? And you never told any of us?"

Jake watched a milk truck clatter down Main Street. He said nothing.

"Listen to me," his brother continued. "I don't want to hear any more of this. I have to get to work. I think you should wrap things up down there, go back to your girlfriend, and get some rest before coming out here. And I think you should really consider therapy, seriously this time."

"Don't you always know what's best."

"And don't go telling the rest of us about this. I'm going to delete this from the transcript. We don't want to get all of us even more upset."

"You do that now."

Jake hung up. He creaked open the phone booth's door and stepped out into the storm. He covered his nose and mouth with his collar and guarded his eyes with his arm. Sand blasted through the air, grit catching in Jake's mustache, passing through his yellow gold lashes to lodge in his eye. He squinted and stumbled blindly toward his motel.

"You can't take her!" he shouted into the storm, shaking his head against the earthen air. "You can't take her away from me."

Jake peered up at restaurant's rafters. All over the ceiling, columns, and support beams, the management had mounted dozens of jackalopes: gray jackrabbit heads with antlers drilled into their skulls. Big jacks, little jacks. Some staring dead ahead, others with views slightly askew, gazing thoughtfully across the expanse of the steak house.

"I ought to get one of these for my girlfriend," Jake said, mentioning her for the third time.

The waitress from the coffee shop smiled. "Jake, hon, a girl doesn't want a jackalope. Get her something nice."

"Aw, yeah. Suppose you're right. Thanks." He smiled gratefully. "You know, I always thought it was kinda strange jackalopes didn't have any other relatives."

She set down her steak knife. "What do you mean? They've got jackrabbits and antelopes."

Jake nodded thoughtfully. "Yeah, but, I mean, why are there only jackalopes? Why not dogalopes or catalopes or rattlesnakealopes?"

She cocked her head. "Well, they do have one cousin. Cantaloupes."

Jake laughed into the back of his fist.

She picked out a saccharin packet and shook it decisively. "Forgive my foolishness."

Jake waved his hand. "No, no—that's pretty good."

"Thank you, thank you. I'll be appearing all week at New Garton's most exciting comedy club, Milk Out Yer Nose."

Jake lowered his head, still chuckling. "Oh, Lord..."

She stirred her tea merrily, the slender, silver spoon swirling ice around the mason jar, tinkling against the glass. "Anyhow," she said, "we should probably be grateful there aren't no more stupid critters with sharp antlers running around than there already is."

Jake raised his eyebrows and nodded.

"It's probably because of your brothers," she said, cutting into her steak. Jake frowned. "You probably always expect there to be lots of something," she explained.

Jake tipped the neck of his beer bottle toward her. "You could be right, ma'am."

She frowned sternly. "I said you could drop this 'ma'am' business," she said. "You call me that while we're here out to dinner, and people'll think I'm the one paying you."

They laughed and looked around the restaurant in mock paranoia. More than one patron turned away, and their laughter quieted.

"Seriously, kid. World must look pretty queer to you boys. Does it seem not right to you: people being all alone?"

"You mean Indies?" Jake laughed. "That's what we call everyone else: 'Indies.' For 'individuals.'"

Her smile said nothing.

"Well, we've tried real hard to each make our lives all separate. I mean, we've all tried to build lives like you and everyone else." Jake paused. He reached into the breadbasket for another butter-soaked slab of Texas toast.

"Except maybe Ally. I mean, he lives up there in Alaska in a cabin he built himself. He hasn't shaved his head. He hasn't gone gay or Jewish or anything."

"Jewish?"

"Yeah, my brother in New York. We even have to call him Jacob."

"My stars. I didn't know you could become Jewish."

"He says he's going to." Jake shrugged. "So, yeah, despite all the different things we've all done, Jacob—my brother in New York—he's the only one of us that changed his name. He doesn't really think it's a change, though, just a switch to his proper name. But I say your name's yours, your name's special, even if you have to share it. He's the only one of us that really got religion. I go to mass with my girlfriend, but it's not a big thing to me."

"You don't like it?"

"No, it's more like—I just don't get it. Even though we've been on our own for years, there's still a lot that just doesn't click for me, you know? World's so full of stuff that just don't make sense to us. Things everyone else is real passionate about. Rituals. I don't even try to understand anymore. I smile or frown like I'm supposed to, go along to make folks happy. Yeah, church. Birthdays. Super Bowl. Arguing about silly songs on the radio or shows on TV. Not walking under ladders or stepping on sidewalk cracks.

"It's funny—the outside world or whatever, everyone thinks they're so unique, so individual. But they all live by all these habits and patterns. People always thought *we* were such identical freaks, but they spend most of their waking hours running around doing great big group things. They march all around in all these elaborate formations, and they pretend not to see them. They may *look* all different, but they *act* just the same."

He lowered his eyes. "Sorry—we don't normally talk about this. Indies like to believe they're Indie. They usually get all worked up if we suggest anything else. Lots of things make Indies upset. I just have to remember them all. But no offense."

She nodded. "Mm-hmm."

"Anyway, you were asking about us. Ah, let's see...so, Jacob is the guy becoming Jewish. Holly's is the gay guy. I'm the regular guy who just wants to marry his girl, open his own garage, and have some kids. Ally is the guy just like our father, looks just like him, except I don't think he'll ever get married. I don't think he's ever even kissed a girl. He was always the most stubborn of all of us. Always worked the hardest. I think he loved Dad the most. Most anyone could.

"Sometimes I just think Ally's ahead of the game. We're still young. Maybe all our trying so hard to be different is just foolish. Some teenage independence thing we'll all grow out of. Maybe we'll all end up like Ally, looking all identical again once we stop trying to be different. Living like how we grew up. They say that's what finally happens in your thirties."

"Everyone becomes their parents," she said.

"Did you?"

She laughed. "Not by a long shot, hon."

"Good. I sure enough don't want to go repeating my father's story." He rapped twice on the wood tabletop and looked at her. "Whatever that story might be."

She sighed.

"I'm sorry." Jake leaned back in his chair. "I'm sorry, that was right pushy of me."

She shook her head and held out her palm. "No, no. It's why we came here. I was just having a nice time playing make-believe, like this was purely a social call. I don't get many of those, Jake. My husband died, you know, and my boy's over at a facility in El Paso. Permanently." She smiled. "So I'm not a very hot property. And I suppose I'm not looking that forward to talking about the past. That's why I was so cold to you there for a while."

"That's all right. I don't want to upset you none."

"You're sweet," she pronounced. "You look like a right nice young fellow. If the rest of you boys turned out nice, maybe your dad had a good side."

"Thanks, but I wouldn't give him too much credit."

She smiled. "Tell you what, kiddo. Let's just finish up our supper here, real nice. Then you can drive me out to the park and I'll tell you what all I know. The park's just gorgeous, up on a hill over town. At night you can see near every star God ever made."

Jake nodded. "It's a deal."

She glanced around the restaurant and smiled apologetically. "I'd rather not get into it all here, anyway." She cocked her head, then burst into a conspiratorial smile. "Jake, you know they got a good Mississippi Mud cake here."

A short drive outside of town, the humble park reached up to the sky. Unpaved switchbacks off the main highway climbed the escarpment, the only natural landmark within eyesight of New Garton. A sandstone plateau topped the ridge, with a small section graveled for parking. Near the cliff's edge, town planners had planted a park bench and a swing set, its chains jangling forlornly in the night breeze.

"You know New Garton's famous?" she asked him. "You're not from just any ole pissant town; we do have historical significance."

"Really? What?"

Jake and the waitress stood beside the bench. Heat lightning flashed distant yellow in the sky. New Garton twinkled below. Outside of town, a freight train inched slowly east.

"Infamous might be more like it. New Garton's where the San Patricios deserted."

"Who?"

"San Patricios. Saint Patrick's Battalion. About 500 Irish guys who ditched the U.S. Army during the Mexican-American War and joined up with the Mexicans. They didn't like the U.S. expansion, and they really didn't like how they treated the Mexicans. They were Catholics, too, and Irishmen back then knew a thing or two about discrimination. So during a battle right around here, they switched sides. They were all hung once the U.S. won the war, won Texas. Don't make it to the history books much."

"Well now." Jake shook his head. "My education was a bit patchy growing up." He looked up. The deep, dark sky loomed massive above them. The abundance of stars dirtied the pitch expanse, as if white sand had been scattered across a black towel. Crowded and busy, the star-field exploded as perfect proof of powers beyond man.

"This is the sky I grew up with," Jake whispered.

She nodded, pacing the gravel's perimeter and looking skyward. "Always gives me chillbumps just looking up at it," she said. "It's easy to be all tough during the day, but at night it's another story." Jake walked slightly behind her.

"You and your brothers real close?" she asked.

"Suppose so. Not like we used to be, though."

"Y'all get together much?"

"Can't say that we do. We see each other one-on-one every now and then, and a couple of times three of us have hooked up, but all four of us haven't been in the same place since we got out on our own."

"Never?"

"Nope. Suppose it's mostly schedules and travel and such. And we're not that big on holidays—we always spend our birthday with our own friends." Jake picked up a flat white pebble and pitched it into the night. "Anyhow, it's not like we really have to be together."

"What do you mean? Y'all read each other's minds or something?"

"No, well—no. Actually, we—it's not that specific. It's like this: Imagine being in a big room with three other people, and your eyes are closed. They're all talking in, I don't know, ancient Mayan. You don't know what anyone is saying, but you can tell about how many people are there, where they're coming from in the room, and if they're happy or sad or whatnot."

"So you feel everything together, like twins?"

"That's kind of a tall tale. What we've got's not regular or predictable, and it's usually not that specific." He laughed. "You should've seen us when puberty hit. One of us would have a dream, you know, and sometimes it would domino all the rest of us. We'd all be up in the middle of the night, washing out our sheets. Trying not to wake up Dad."

She looked at him quizzically.

"He didn't like us wasting our, ah, fluids. No sex 'til marriage, either."

"I didn't know Jake was a Holy Roller."

"Naw, it wasn't really about Jesus. It was more like, it was special. It was—yourself. Us."

She nodded. "Didn't this all get a little strange, what with having a gay brother?"

"Nope, it's not that...detailed. Like last tonight, f'rinstance, I know one of us had some real awful nightmare. I don't know what it was. I just felt some cold fist reach right into my heart and grab hold. As strong as I felt the dream, I still don't know which of us had it."

"Well, I hope everyone's all right." They walked farther and she whispered, "What's it like being a part of all y'all?"

"I remember times when it was good," he said. "When we'd be cutting brush or hauling rocks, off doing some chore, off far away somewhere where Dad wasn't around. We'd be in the sun, and we'd move just like an assembly line. We knew exactly what each of us could do best and how to divvy up the job into four parts. And then we'd start going, and we'd just be tearing into it, running back and forth with buckets of water, or passing tools, tossing them through the air, relaying shovels of dirt, sawed-off tree branches. It was like we were all just one big sweaty, muddy machine. You'd turn and someone would always be there, holding his hand out with whatever you needed. He was always there for you. Always.

"When we started sneaking out at night, one or two of us always stayed behind to keep watch on Dad. Two or three of us, we'd go running through the woods in starlight, not needing any path because we all just knew how to follow each other, knew each other's movements before we moved. It didn't feel like running in line. It felt like you were some kind of connected, legless snake flying through the air. We'd come to some new crest of a hill, and stand back-to-back, take in the view from all four directions all at once. It was like there was enough of us to see the whole world at once. You never had to worry about watching your back.

"It was like being completely a part of something, but at the same time you felt more individual than ever in your life. There was no problem between 'Me' and 'Us.' We only made each other stronger. We were this wild pack, but we weren't animals. It was like being lost and found at the same time."

"Y'all would've made a mean offensive line."

"Actually we all did pretty poorly in team sports. We were so used to being coordinated together, we could never figure out how to connect with strangers. It was like they weren't speaking the same language as us. Like they weren't talking at all. But Dad didn't like us playing with the town Indies, anyway. And even when we lived at the service station, the Indies didn't want to play with us."

He chuckled softly. "But we did just all get together for a video conference."

"Video conference?"

"For the will—that's when Dad told us."

She cleared her throat. "What all did he tell you?"

Jake eyed her directly. "Growing up, he always said that our mom died giving birth. He said that we pretty much killed her. He told us he buried her behind the house. That was one of his big paranoid soapboxes, how the funeral industry, coffins, and embalming were all big scams. There's no law requiring you to spend thousands of dollars on death rituals."

Jake breathed deeply. "Dad left us this—message right before he died. Said one of us was not his son. One of us was not a brother. One of us was the son of a woman who lives back east. She's named Brett Ashley—and he practically dared us to go find her. She's real—we called her. She hung up on us."

"That doesn't surprise me."

"It didn't make any sense. We're quadruplets. Of course we're related. But her reaction got us suspicious. She hung up when we mentioned his name. And she said, "None of you *four*," like she knew about us. Like she has some connection to us. So maybe there's something there. Maybe there's some crazy truth to all this."

He laughed softly. "We're kind of an unusual family. So, well, we're all going to see if she'll meet us in person. I came here to see what I could find out first. In case—it's about me."

Jake looked at his feet. He and the waitress had wandered far from the gravel into dirt and sandstone peppered with sagebrush and cacti. He stepped a few feet ahead, giving her space.

"Well," she sighed, "I can tell you what I do know. It may not be what you want to hear. In fact, none of this may even fit together."

Jake turned around. "Don't worry," he said. "Anything

would be a big help."

"Well, all right," she said dubiously. "Where do I start?"

"I know about the midwifery. And the rest."

"Well, that's common knowledge in this town. Yes, once upon a time, I was a little hippie girl, starry-eyed and stupid, but not as stupid as some. I'd gone out to California, lived in a commune, and learned to make yogurt and eat dirt and use herbs and midwife babies. I came back to New Garton when my momma got sick. I took care of her for three years and never did manage to leave again.

"During that time another know-it-all kid moved back to town. He had gotten all these scholarships to go to med school. But he finally decided it was too 'establishment' and moved back here. More like he got kicked out for cooking up too many drugs.

"Now, he hated the 'establishment' but liked it when it paid his bills. He moved back here to live off his daddy's money. We fell in together—two hotshots who'd seen the world but came back. He thought we could make our mark on the world here at home, with a little underground, alternative health care. I worked at the movie theater during the day, then helped him out at night. Eventually we got married. I had a son. We built up a whole little life."

Jake digested this, mentally comparing notes with what he'd learned so far from others.

"We grew herbs and drugs, patched up stabbings or gunshots no one wanted the rest of town to know about, same thing for babies. Sometimes it was society girls who needed an abortion. Lord, they came from ten counties around! Or the family hid the pregnancy—they came to us for the childbirth, then we took the baby over to the orphanage in Esperanza. We also got a lot of hippie traffic. There was a commune out near the Hermann River, plus lots came down from the university in El Paso. They came to us because they couldn't afford a doctor, or they wanted to do it natural, or they didn't want any records. We only trusted each other in those days.

"He had plenty of money, and people paid us what they could. We did a lot of barter. But that's not what you want to know about.

"Yes, of course, your father lived here. Yes, he had a wife, but no one ever saw much of her. She wasn't from around here.

He was just about the only one that ever came into town. She did get pregnant eventually. But your dad wouldn't have nothing to do with the doctor at the clinic. So we went out to their place once for a checkup. Lord, she was huge. We thought twins, but we didn't know for sure. Your dad didn't even trust us much, ended up chasing us off and saying he could handle the delivery himself.

"Now, long about this same time a couple of kids from the commune out on the Hermann came through in their van. Stupid as a box of rocks, both of them. They camped out near us, waiting for her to give birth. He was always stoned, and she was some silly, rich Yankee girl who thought she'd have a little adventure dropping out and being a hippie. Reckon she got more adventure than she hoped for."

"But—my dad?"

"Your dad came into town for supplies right after the hippie girl had her baby—a boy. I asked Jake how his wife was doing, and he looked at me like he was gonna kill me. I tried to lighten him up. I told him how we'd be ready for her 'cause we just had delivered this hippie girl's boy.

"Well, that didn't make your dad none the happier. He just stormed off from me, furious as all get-out."

"I still don't see—" Jake said.

"Hush up, child, and let me finish. And don't go telling anyone else about this. The hippie couple took their baby, left to go back east. Having a kid made her wise up real quick. She knew she'd need her family money to support him.

"They didn't make it. Their van was found about twenty miles outside of town in the desert. Her boyfriend had been killed. It got all written up in the paper. Big scandal, big Sunday School lesson of what happens to nice girls who become hippies.

"Jake, hon, there wasn't no baby in the van. The newspaper, the police, no one said anything about a baby, no one knew he'd been born, and of course we couldn't talk about what we knew. We'd go to jail.

"Next time Jake came into town, he told the sheriff his wife had died in childbirth. Sheriff had the county medical examiner look at the body. He confirmed it, and Jake, yeah, he buried her back behind his cabin. Now, Jake's wife died, but her babies hadn't. Your father said she'd had four. He was so proud. He knew that quads happened once in—"

"Eleven million births."

"Of course you'd know that. He was so proud, like he'd created his own little army. But Jake moved away that winter. Said he needed to find some safer place to raise his boys.

"Kiddo, I don't know if this has anything to do with you. That hippie girl had a boy who disappeared, and I didn't say nothing about it. Your dad said his wife had four boys. Your father is obviously Jake, not the hippie boy. Just look at you. But after your dad left, well, you know he became kind of a local legend. Kids would dare each other to go out to his old cabin at night—no one else ever moved into it.

"Now this is just town gossip, but rumor got round that some kids went out there one full moon on a dare and they— Jake, they dug up your mother's grave. This was years after the medical examiner had looked at her. It's horrible, I know, but kids do horrible things sometimes. But Jake, listen. The story these kids told is that there was a baby in there with her. There hadn't been one when the examiner dug her up. I don't know what it means. Maybe she really had quints and one died. Jake kept it and then reburied it with her. Maybe something happened to the hippie girl's baby, and somehow Jake ended up burying the baby with his wife. I can't imagine it all, and I don't want to. Maybe it's all coincidence. Stranger things—"

A sharp rattle cut the night's quiet.

"Jake!" she hissed. "Freeze!"

"I know," he whispered. Jake squinted, trying to see the rattler, its noise quieter but still steady. He inched backward. The snake shot out from beside him and bit into the back of Jake's ankle.

"Ow!" he shouted. "Fuck!"

"Jake!" She rushed over to him. She kicked the snake away with a loud "Scat!"

"Look out," Jake gasped.

"It'll be okay, kid," she said. Jake slumped onto her shoulder. "I had the sense to wear my boots tonight. Shouldn't've drug you up here in those tennies. Here—" She sat him down on the bench. "I can drive you down to the doc's." She knelt in the gravel.

"Aren't you going to suck it out?"

She looked at him sternly. "Not on the first date, sweetie."

ONE OF THESE THINGS IS NOT LIKE THE OTHER

"But—"

"Child." She sat her purse on the bench and snapped it open, pulling out a small, yellow plastic box. "I've got an extractor. You don't want me adding my germs to the badness you already got in you. Guess your old man didn't know everything."

She opened the box and set it on the ground beside them. Squinting, she pushed Jake's pants leg above his knee and traced her finger along the bite mark. "There he is." She replaced her finger with a small plastic tube and finger-pump, and pumped the handle with her thumb.

Jake gasped as the suction drew his skin up into the plastic tube: a rude, mechanical hickey.

"Jake, hon, you gotta stay calm. This won't get it all out, and we don't want the venom spreading around your system. So calm yourself best you can, okay? Then we'll get you right to the doc's for some antivenin."

She clicked the extractor into its plastic case. "There." She fished a paisley scarf from her purse and wrapped it around Jake's leg, an inch above the wound.

"Shouldn't that be tighter?" Jake asked.

"Jake. You want gangrene?" She snapped her purse shut and slung it over her shoulder. "Now give me your hand."

She helped Jake back to his truck.

"No cracks about women drivers," she warned as he handed her his truck's keys. "Remember I'm saving your ass."

Jake slammed the passenger door shut. "Thank you," he gasped.

"What?"

Jake winced as the truck bounced along the unpaved road. "For what you told me."

"You're welcome. Not that I'm very proud of any of it. Now Jake, don't get excited."

Jake gasped as they pitched around a switchback, throwing him against the truck cab's passenger door.

"Jake, I saw that picture you had with you at the coffee shop. That woman—that's the hippie girl. Cleaned up, but that's her."

"That's Brett Ashley."

"I figured as much. I don't know where all this will take you, but I'm telling you because—because I feel like telling the truth about those years for a change. You don't look anything like her.

"I know. I don't see anything, either." He swallowed painfully, gripping the door handle. "But it feels right."

"So you going on after her?"

"Yeah. I've got to. Maybe it's some mix-up. Maybe that's her baby buried out with my mom. She can tell us what her connection is to Dad, and what happened to her baby, and if it relates to us."

They pulled up outside a small adobe bungalow. The yard was decorated with a flowering cactus garden and cast-resin figures of cows playing hide-and-seek in children's clothes. A floodlight bathed the truck in white. Jake and the waitress squinted.

"Hello? Who's out there?" called a silhouette from the front porch.

She rolled down her window and shielded her eyes from the light. "It's me, Doc. We got a rattler bite here. Help me get him inside."

The doctor shuffled down his driveway.

She turned to Jake, taking his hand in hers. "Now Jake, you gotta promise to keep me posted on the mystery. I hope I was able to help you out. I'm glad I got to know you." She squeezed his fingers.

Jake nodded. "I much appreciate it. It was good to meet you, too. You've helped make my past more real."

"The past," she murmured sadly. "Is it ever real?" She put on a strained smile. The doctor tapped on the glass behind Jake's head. Jake jumped, turned, and stared at the doctor. She reached across Jake and unlocked his door.

Jake sat on the edge of his motel bed. He stubbed out his cigarette in the amber glass ashtray on the comforter beside him. He dragged his palms across the comforter, wiping them dry. The porn movie's credits crawled up the TV screen.

Well now I feel even worse. Jake sighed. He bent down and pulled his boxers up to his knees. He paused, turning his ankle around and inspecting the bandage. *Guess I got my battle scar.*

He looked over at his packed bags near the door. The message light flashed on his phone, probably from his girlfriend. *I can't tell her about the snake, or what I'm doing next. I can't explain myself to her now.*

He fell flat back on the bed, lifted up his butt, and wiggled the rest of the way back into his boxers. Rolling over on the bed, he twisted sideways and pulled his feet up on the bed. He looked up sheepishly at the open tequila bottle on his nightstand and wriggled forward on the bed. He grabbed the bottle and took another swig, smacking his lips.

Gingerly he swung his feet up, beside, and back behind him, rolling onto his belly on the center of the bed. With one hand hovering outstretched over the floor, he wriggled his torso forward, off the bed, toward the chair holding his guitar. He stretched, torso curving upward like a snake. He grabbed the guitar's neck and lifted it up above his head. Bracing himself against the floor, he scooted backward until back on the bed.

"Whew."

He rolled over onto his back and swung his feet around, propping his bandaged foot on the chair. He slipped the guitar into his arms and plucked a few strings, twisted the tuning screws.

Jake strummed, humming along. He struck a chord with extra vigor and froze. He snapped his neck from side to side like a go-go girl and giggled. His playing slowed as he changed tunes and hummed, occasionally singing a thin, whispered word or phrase.

"You're not just a friend,
And only you know me.
You are my brother."

Jake snorted a derisive laugh set down the guitar. *Brother. Brothers. Oh brother.* He reached for the tequila. *Now what do we want, Jakey-Jake?* He drew from the bottle. *Do we want brothers? Or do we want a mother?*

ALASKA

Unblinking, Jake stared at the screen of his new Internet appliance—dull gray squares where there had been the images of his brothers. The video conference was over. In his hands he held the webcam. The will was read. His father was dead.

Jake set the webcam down on the table. He looked over his shoulder, surveying the silent cabin. He returned to the cool screen.

A dialog box fluttered onto view. Jake blinked. *No active conference parties*, the message read. The screen offered Jake a pair of options: *Disconnect* and *Open New Connection*.

Jake snorted. His hand thrust out from his lap, but paused in the air above the mouse. He flicked his finger, skittering the mouse across the wood kitchen table.

The message persisted. Jake's face wrinkled, his mop of russet curls creeping down his furrowed brow and hanging above his eyes. He reached under the table and groped for the smooth, cool cables. He stretched around the table and eyed the outlet interrupting the raw wood of the cabin's wall. He yanked a cord, creating a quick blue spark, and bent to survey the ax-cut table's unfinished underside. Nothing had caught.

"Hmpf."

He inspected the disconnected contraption, its purr now silenced. A sneer rustled Jake's bushy red beard. He shook his head.

That's all I want to hear out of you.

He reached behind and unplugged or unscrewed everything he found. He hauled the mess into his living room and unceremoniously dumped the heap of green plastic, curly cables, and rubber-coated antennas onto the beige coyote skin covering the sofa.

Still got the crate and straw out in the cabin. I'll just take you right back to the supermart, good as new. Get my money back for something useful.

Dumped on the couch, the machine looked defeated, an unsuccessful intruder into an environment of furs and hides, mounted heads, antlers, and fish.

"I don't know what the hell Daddy was doing with all that stuff."

Jake remembered not long ago, only a few weeks after he'd first picked up the Internet appliance. He'd complained to the crowd at the tavern.

"What's he see in all that computer shit anyway? Not what he taught us."

No one in the tavern had offered him an answer.

"I don't want to 'chat' with someone in New Zealand. I don't like movies. I don't read newspapers. You guys tell me the news when I come to town. It's always bad or someone else's business. Library in Fairbanks got more books than I can ever read. I can get all my gear and provisions in town or with catalogs. Why shell out for a machine, just so I can be all special, being on that Internet? Catalogs are free. And if I buy new boots from a computer, I still have to go down and pick them up at the post office, so it's not any easier for me."

"It makes me feel less alone," the woman working the bar had said. "Living here, you know?"

Jake had offered no reply.

"But that probably don't bother you much," she'd noted.

"There's a lot more out there," a man down the bar had said, sidling up to the stool beside Jake. "You wouldn't believe these girls," he'd growled under his breath. "You can talk to them, tell them what to do, and they'll do it. Anything. And they got cameras that go everywhere." Leering, his eyes had gleamed over his beer foam.

Jake had pushed away from the bar, grabbing his pack. "Got everything I need already."

All in the tavern had rolled their eyes. They'd heard that before.

"I just bought it because my daddy did. When I was down to see him on Easter, he had a whole wall built up of the stuff.

Computers and web browsers and CB radios and 8-track recorders and everything you can think of."

"Why'd he get all that, Jake?"

"Don't know. Figured they must've changed if he likes that stuff now." He had snorted in disgust. "But I hate it. Don't want people's messages coming into my house. Don't want to crawl around in a web. And you know what color it is? Neon green. All they had was that or pink." He fished a strip of venison jerky from his chest pocket.

"When's it going to put more rabbits in my traps? Skin a deer? Chop wood?"

"Well, hell, Jake, if you don't want it—my kids been pestering me for one something awful."

"Didn't say I was going to get rid of it. Daddy's still got his."

He unlatched an oil lantern from its hook in the rafters, set it on the table, and lit the wick. He suited up and tightened his snowshoes. Grabbing the lantern, he tramped outside of his warm home and into the frigid dark.

Jake shook out the last of the dog food. The pack of huskies and wolf hybrids crowded around their bowls. A few looked up from feeding at the sound of the kennel's gate clinking locked. Jake left them. He wadded up the empty bag between his mittened fists and carried it to the trash-burning barrel. He shoved it in and clanged down the lid.

Jake stood, staring at his trash while the snow gently dusted his shoulders. Wild sounds surrounded him: the river rushing down the hill behind the cabin, wolves howling in the distance, the dogs crunchy-snuffling behind him. Jake held up his lantern and looked at his reflection in the cabin's back window, ominously lit from the side.

I look like a ghost, Jake thought. *Like I'm dead.*

"Hey, Dad," he whispered. He set down the lantern on top of the barrel and the face in the glass disappeared.

Jake turned to his right, looking over at where the garden was in spring. Two mounds glowed blue white in the moonlight. It was comforting to see two instead of the usual one: his mother's snow-covered grave now joined by his father's. Fresh snowfall had almost completely covered the more recent memorial. Above, aurora flashed bright, furious sheets of green and yellow. The shifting curtains of excited ions glowered malevolently, rippling slow-motion in the heavens. A scream frozen across the sky, pained and silent like Jake.

Light followed Jake back to bed. The air of his room glowed with diffused moonlight reflecting off the snow. Pouring through the window above his head, the persistent twilight cast a faint blue rectangle, undulating across the curving logs. Orange cinders glowed through the slits in a squat iron stove, crackling and popping in the corner.

Jake burrowed deeper into bed, hiding under the pelts and quilts. His exhales heated the air, dank and claustrophobic. Jake slid a hand under his thermal shirt. He crept upward, touching chest hair, feeling muscles rise and fall. He scraped a fingertip across a nipple. His head felt light, breathing his own fumes. He placed his palm on his forehead, digging fingers into the wavy mess of coarse hair, massaging his scalp, curls twisting between his fingers. He ran his fingertips over his eyebrows, eyelids, lashes. Nose, nostrils, upper lip, lips, teeth, jaw, ears. One hand caressed his face in all its detail while his other furiously masturbated.

Jake tried to hide in the post office, but the limited facility offered little sanctuary. It wasn't even a building, merely a reception window inside the narrow hallway that ran from the grocery store back to the bathrooms shared with the gun shop. There was a pay phone mounted next to the window and a rickety card table below, neither of which could successfully shadow the tall redhead. He arched his arms and shoulders around the phone and glared at anyone who approached the table, no matter if their hands were full of packages and labels. All afternoon he'd trudged back and forth between the tavern and the post office, feeding the phone Susan B. Anthony dollars. Soon the post office would close, and he didn't have any answers yet. He dropped in a coin and dialed Oregon again, the number that once was his father's.

"Hello?"

"Glowie!"

"Yeah—damn, Ally, I told you I don't like those old names."

"I'm sorry. You're finally home."

"I felt like I should get back here."

"Been calling you all day. Didn't you feel me?"

"Maybe. I don't know. I was at the church all day with the ladies, unpacking Dad's stuff for their bazaar. It was all noisy and so many people—I thought I felt one of us, but I wasn't sure."

"You didn't know it was me? I knew you were still at Dad's, but that was about all I could tell."

"Yeah. We all seem to be getting kind of quiet since Dad—"

"I feel you all the time. I always feel us."

His brother cleared his throat. "I'm just exhausted, I guess. Sorry. There's just, there's been a lot of work here for me to do."

"Sounds like Dal's been real busy down in Texas."

"Busy nearly getting himself killed. He knows better than to get bit by a rattler. What's up with him? You've been getting Enwycie's carbons?"

"I got them all in my mail this week."

"Yeah? What do you think about it all? All these stories, damn. Kidnapped hippie babies and a dead baby buried with Mom? It's totally fucked up."

"I got the package you sent. With the picture."

"Great. What do you think of her, our Miss Brett Ashley?"

One of the town kids waddled down the hall past Jake, eyeing him warily from under his snowsuit's furry hood. Jake turned away and faced the wall. "I meant the picture of *us*," he whispered urgently.

"Oh yeah, that was a trip. I figured we should all have copies since it's just about our only childhood picture."

"I don't need a picture. I remember those days perfectly. I think about them all the time."

Jake listened as the pause on the line stretched into silence.

"Right," his brother finally said. "So, what about Brett Ashley?"

"Did you send her the picture of us?"

"Yes."

"Good. Now we need to go out and see her. I think this could fix everything." Jake looked down at the phone cord twisted around his fingers.

"Jesus," his brother sighed. "I don't know if our family can be fixed. Maybe at least we can get some answers. Find out if there was any truth in what Dad was saying."

"Dad's gone. There's just us now, and we've got to get our shit together. Our lives."

"I'm sorry—mm—I don't understand what you're saying."

"I've got to talk to you."

His brother was silent. Jake peeked nervously down the hall. The grocery store's lights flickered off one by one.

"Holly, listen up. They're closing here, and I gotta go, and my phone at home comes and goes. Aurora's been heavy this week. Okay, now, so, listen. You've got to come up here after you're done down in Oregon. We need to go to New York together."

"What?"

"We gotta talk. In person. Get an airship up to Fairbanks, and I'll come pick you up from the landing field. I'll pay for the ticket. Don't tell the rest of us."

"Ally, what the hell—"

"Just do it, okay? For me? It's about Dad."

"Why can't we—"

"I can't! It's about why Dad died. And where we go from here. You have to come here! I need you."

"Okay," his brother murmured.

"Don't tell the others," Jake said. "Send me a telegram at the post office with your arrival time."

"Hey, Jake." An old man stuck his head out the post office window. He waved his arm at Jake. "Finish up. I want to get home."

Jake nodded.

"I gotta go, brother. I'll see you up here."

Jake grabbed the microphone with both hands, eyes closed, his freckled nose wrinkled in emotion. He leaned forward and howled, "Yooooooou're not just a friend."

The woman behind the bar winced. "When did you let him talk you into doing this at *lunch*?" she whispered. Her husband shrugged and fiddled with the knobs on the karaoke machine, turning up the reverb and vocal effects, the volume down.

Jake's song reached a triumphant crescendo. "And only you know me!" One of the fixed-income alcoholics, who'd been nursing a pint since midmorning, cheered Jake from a barstool. His Inuit buddy beside him tossed a handful of holographic pull tabs in the air, the national lottery raining down as disco confetti.

Jake hushed to a dramatic whisper, opening his eyes. The neon beer sign behind him cast a fiery aura around Jake's face. He took one hand off the microphone and solemnly pointed to the empty air in front of him. "You are my brother..."

Jake lowered his head and wiped his eyes. Someone in the far corner of the tavern clapped. Behind the bar, the bartender shot her husband a warning look. Jake stumbled off the packing flat that served as a makeshift stage. He steadied himself against the jukebox, and grabbed his pitcher of beer off the top of the pinball machine. Retreating to his corner table, he sipped straight from the pitcher, eyes wet. Foam soaked his beard.

Jake waved at the bartender for another. He patted the chest pocket of his flannel shirt and pulled out a pencil. He smoothed out a bar napkin in front of him. He drew two small circles and filled them in black.

"Jake, you a singer *and* an artist?" joked the bartender.

"Fuck off, sweetie," he replied. She dropped the pitcher down roughly, foam sloshing over the lip. Jake jerked the napkin away to keep it dry. He mopped up the mess with his cuff. When satisfied that the surface was dry, he carefully laid the napkin back down and returned to his diagram.

Above one black circle he wrote "Dad + Mom." The other he labeled "Hippie Girl (Brett Ashley) + Boyfriend." Below he drew five more black dots and placed a larger oval around them. Over the oval he wrote, "Boys." From four of the boy-dots he drew a solid line connecting them to "Dad + Mom." The remaining boy-dot he linked via a dotted line to "Hippie Girl (Brett Ashley) + Boyfriend."

Now, there's the dead baby they found. If that was... He drew an X through one of the four boy-dots under "Dad + Mom."

And if you came over to replace him... From the fifth boy-dot, the one linked to Brett Ashley, he drew a solid arrow pointing to the dot he had crossed out.

That could be you. That would be okay. He added some letters and a new circle.

"Hey Jake!" called out the bartender's husband. "You

writing the Great Alaskan Novel over there?"

Jake stared down hard at his napkin, committing it to memory:

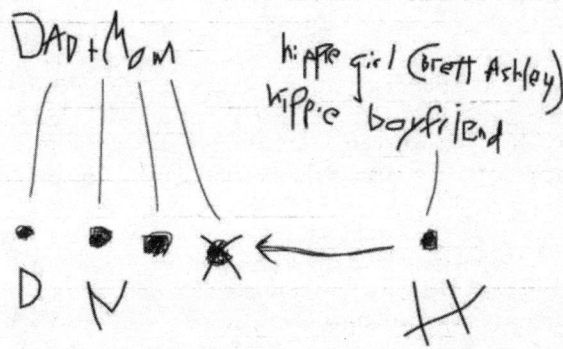

"Nothin'," he said, crumpling up the napkin. "Just makin' plans for my brother's visit."

"You gonna bring him here to meet everyone?"

Jake wiped his mouth and eyes, shaking his head. He pushed the pitcher away from him. "I gotta get to the post office before he closes."

Jake slit open the telegram with his thumbnail. It read: "Arriving Friday. Alaskan #224 3:10 p.m." Jake nodded.

"Finally," he murmured. He folded the paper, placing it in his parka's chest-zip pocket. He started his truck and looked over his shoulder to exit the grocery store lot. A moose had wandered onto the other side of the road. Jake grunted and eased out, rumbling past the impassive moose and heading down the highway home. He coughed and wiped his watery eyes. He couldn't clearly see the road in the dim light.

He pulled into the turnoff to the Phrixus Compound. Jake shook his head at the survivalists' underground homes, ventilation shafts poking through the snow. *World end yet? You all happy down there all snug together?*

Jake remembered tents they'd made as boys, sleeping huddled together under itchy gunnysacks. He stopped the truck. He left the engine running and fell onto the steering wheel, punching his fist into the seat cushion beside him. Tears gathered and ran down the steering column.

He sat upright and made a growling sound. He shook his head violently, collected himself, and made a U-turn, out of the turnoff and toward his empty home.

Jake slid out the storage bin mounted underneath the kitchen table and pulled out an old quilt. Blotches of grease and blood marred its pink-and-blue squares, yet its embroidered daisies smiled on. He spread the quilt over the table, laying the clean side against the wood, and smoothed out the wrinkles.

In the mudroom, Jake looked through his shopping bags from town. Inspecting his new purchases, he noted that the shears needed oiling and polishing before going out to the shed, and the two cast-iron skillets needed seasoning. He fished out plastic-wrapped bundles of T-shirts and briefs, stuffed them inside the neck of his fleece vest and, holding the hem of the vest closed, grabbed the remaining bag by its twine handles.

He set the bag at the foot of the table. Reaching into his vest, he grabbed the bundled shirts and underwear and pitched them up into his lofted bedroom. He hung his vest on a peg near the mudroom door and put more wood in the kitchen stove.

Sitting at the table, he probed the bag, pulled out the new pair of snowshoes, and set them on the table. Jake patted his callused palm on the kitchen tabletop, happy to have regained the workspace. The caning of the shoes gave off a faint dusty, yet sweet, smell, like sassafras candy.

"Hope Glowfishie even remembers how to walk in these," he muttered. He cocked an eyebrow at the snow-ox head on the column between the kitchen and living room.

"What do you think, Prince? They use snowshoes down in Hollywood?" The fox's glass eyes didn't blink.

Jake chuckled and shook his head. He prepped the snowshoes one at a time, blowing dust off, wiping it clean with a damp sponge, then drying it with a towel.

He held a shoe close to his face, peering at the woven caning. Upon finding a flaw—a loose or cracked spot—he ran a fingertip across to confirm the mar. Frowning, he kept his finger on the error and set the snowshoe back on the table. With his free right hand he grabbed the shellac and held the bottle steady with his palm and three fingers; his thumb and index finger loosened the lid. He pulled off the lid, its attached brush dripping sticky, translucent fluid, and scraped the excess against the bottle's lip. Lifting his left-hand finger off the flaw, he coated it with glue and pressed the tip of his thumbnail tightly against the loose cane. He blew gently until the glue dried, searching for the next fault.

The phone clanged. Jake jumped at the noise he hadn't heard for days. He growled in exasperation and stared hard at the current fault, so as not to forget its location. He wiped wet glue from his fingertips on a rag and pushed from the table. Lumbering into the main room, he grabbed the phone from its cubbyhole in the bookshelf wall.

"What!?"

"Hello, Mr. Barnes? This is Brett Ashley."

Jake scowled, breathing heavy. His eyebrows furrowed, then relaxed.

"You're her?"

"Are you the young man I spoke to previously?"

"No, no ma'am. We've never spoken directly."

"And you are the Jake Barnes..." She breathed in deeply, inhale hissing across time zones, "...in Alaska?"

"Yes'm."

"Your brother who's been taking care of things in Oregon, he wrote that he was coming to see you, and I should contact him here.

"He don't get here 'til tomorrow."

"I see. He told me you were all traveling cross-country, journeying back east, and you hoped to meet me. To understand why your late father had a picture of me in his possessions?"

The hair on Jake's arms bristled despite the stove's heat.

"Is this correct?"

"Yes'm. We're all hoping to figure out what Dad was talking about. What we have to do with you. Who we all really are."

"That's a lot of questions coming from someone to whom I have not even been properly introduced. You are very forward young men."

"I didn't mean to be rude."

"Yes, I believe you. If you're anything like your brother—

the one I spoke to, in Oregon, although I believe he said he lives in California?"

"Yes'm. Hollywood."

"Really? Well, if you're his brother, I should be able to trust you. That's why I was calling him, to let him know I will welcome meeting him, and any or all of you that also care to come out. And I will share my stories with you."

"Really? You want to see us?"

"I have to apologize, when you first contacted me, I was quite rude. When I heard his voice, I had that feeling as in a nightmare of everything repeating, things I've been through happening again. And he did continue to call me. At first I wouldn't speak to him. Then he sent me a photograph of you boys when you were teenagers, swimming—"

"I know that picture."

"Yes. Well. He also sent me an article from my old church newsletter about myself that your father apparently had kept. Your brother said he was coming out to this part of the country on business and would I see him? It was a flimsy ruse, but I appreciated the effort. He also sent me a current picture of himself. If he grew his hair and beard out, he would be the exact reflection of the Jake Barnes I knew."

"That's how I look."

"Pardon?"

"I've got a beard and hair."

"I see. Well, at that point I was forced to realize you obviously were the sons of Jake Barnes, and this was not some cruel joke."

"We don't joke about this, ma'am. He worked hard to raise us. He was all the world we knew for a long time."

"Yes...and that is precisely why I didn't want to speak with you. Your brother, however, can be very persuasive. Very charming."

Jake smiled. "Glowie's a sweetheart."

"Pardon?"

"Oh sorry. We have nicknames for each other."

"I see. Well. Of course you would, seeing as how you all have the—"

"Same name."

"Yes. But it seems your brothers are referred to by the city in which they reside?"

"Yes'm. We do that, too."

"How very practical. I hope you are practical as well, because you could be in danger."

"What do you mean?"

"You are all obviously sons of Jake Barnes. But he says one of you is not. It may—or it may not—be difficult to believe that he's telling the truth. And even if it's not true, the mere idea of it does not bode well for whichever one of you is not an authentic son of Jake Barnes. Mind you, I do not trust Jake Barnes. But even if he's not telling the truth, it may have nevertheless set things in motion. Things that have involved me. Things I should take care not to ignore.

"That man—your father—devastated my life once. I am determined not to allow a repeat performance, whether orchestrated from the grave or via his progeny."

"His what?"

"Sons."

"We don't want to destroy no one. We're just all trying to find out who we are."

She sighed. "Your father said I have your answers? That one of you is my son?"

"Yes'm."

"Yet you are all identical, obviously born together, obviously his sons, yes?"

"Mm-hmm."

"Well, I did not give birth to four boys. And I certainly never had intimate relations with your father."

"But you said he ruined your life?"

"He did. But that is my story for now. Never underestimate of what men are capable."

"It doesn't make any sense."

"It doesn't have to. Real life rarely does."

Jake sighed irritably and wiped his forehead. "I don't feel so good. This is all making my head hurt."

For the first time, she laughed. "Pain. You have no idea."

"What?"

"Good evening—Mister Barnes."

She hung up. Jake scowled and stumbled over to the table, staring at the snowshoes. He shuffled over to the cupboard, grabbing the bottle of whiskey and a mug. He opened the bottle and carried it into the living room, leaving the mug behind, and collapsed on the sofa.

"Damn, I wish you were here already," he muttered. "Hurry on to me."

The force of my love is unstoppable. The force of my love knows no margin. My love rips through earth and sky. My love slices open your skin, breaks apart your sternum, and takes in your heart.

There is no love like that of a father for a son. Don't believe anyone who tells you any different, who fills you with spurious reason. A man's love for a woman is something that makes you feel complete. But feeling whole is merely an oblique way of gazing upon your ego. In narcissistic reflection, your lack is the focus of your introspection. When you regard the woman you love, and you feel love for how she differs from you, you are actually feeling self-pity for those very things with which you are not imbued. Loving a woman is a torturous self-love, which strengthens no man.

A son, however, is inexorably you. A treasure, in many ways even more so. You are faced with an overwhelming presence of yourself, a horrifying majesty into which you can do nothing but delve. You weaken. You are faced with something so beautiful, majestic, and awesome, you can do nothing but fall on your knees before it, crying and shrieking. You humble yourself; you offer yourself up. That is true love, my dear pup.

And what makes this love greater than any other is this: it is not returned; away it is pissed. The true test of this love — what fires it, hardens it — is that it is not returned in force. A realization slowly grows that the son never will fully embrace his source. Forever a father will enact the lover unrequited. He'll be the back-door woman, the science-class nerd ogling his prom-queen lab partner, the shopping mall schlep who smoothes his lanolin-slicked hair and nibbles breath mints yet never accrues more than looks of contempt from the women to whom he sells shoes. The father knows this is his relationship role: he is forever the one weak, desperate, hopeless. The wife, the patsy, the mistress. Incessantly loving with all his passion, dedication, and ferocity, and praying some day his love's strength will inspire reciprocity.

I realized this, and yet my love persisted. I loved selflessly and unconditionally, despite being resisted.

And my adoration advanced into an action less about an adored and increasingly about the adoring. I loved my loving, less my beloved. I loved my love. I loved myself.

ONE OF THESE THINGS IS NOT LIKE THE OTHER

Love is hopelessness. The sole real love is hopeless. Only the strongest souls are suited for it. It is a solo scene. Some soliloquy of supreme isolation. Loving solidifies solitude; love solely shouts of existential distance.

Still, there is a single supreme advantage to this love. It is a love that actually appreciates no envy. A love actually so adamantine and acutely actualized; a wife, lady, or gay buttboy is unable to affray its absolutism. Absolutely nothing can annihilate such adulation.

I acquired this ardor in an affiliation fourfold.

Females feel love for all their offspring, for females feel love ad infinitum. Love fills their feelings as a feature of their physical functioning; their love is fragile and frail. Females feast in a sphere of love; it forms their fluids and flesh. It is profane. It is familiar. A man's fondness and affection flows not freely; a man's love has to be forcibly shoveled from unformed earth. It requires fervid force for a man to feel love. Work and concentration behoove a man's love, for it is like light, finely focused and fixed fitly through a carefully ground magnifying lens. It is coal-firmed, fired, and forged for many lunar phases into finely cut diamond.

I constructed a world of love. Culled from chaos, love's comfort cradled me. The nocturnal crescent cried coruscating tears of love. Daybreak's crystalline kisses of carmine and crimson streaked the sky, causing me to awaken before a cosmic canvas of love.

I knew more love than any man who's ever lived.

You could have had even more.

Jake opened his eyes, sighed. He swung his legs over the side of the bed, blinked, and rubbed his forehead. He stared at the floor, his father's dream lingering in his mind.

His phone rang.

"Hey. I know it's early, but I felt you were up."

"Yeah."

"I need to give you the call-in number for the conference call. Got a pen?"

"Yeah."

"If you've been reading my carbons, you know Dal has been coming up with some pretty hard-to-swallow stories from down in Texas. I think it's time we all heard from this waitress ourselves, so I got her and Dal to agree to a conference call Tuesday at—ten your time. When she gets off her morning shift tomorrow. The number is 1-877-555-2696. Participant passcode is 679876. You get all that?"

"Yeah," Jake sighed.

"Is Holly up? I can't get a feel for him."

"Glowie's on his way here probably."

"What?"

"He's flying up here today."

"No, what did you call him?"

"Huh? Nothing. I don't know. You woke me up. I'm sleepy."

"Don't play that sweet and simple act with me. I can feel you're up to something. Like things are coming that we can't prevent happening. What is it?"

"Holly's just coming up here, that's all. We're going to come out there together. I talked to Brett Ashley yesterday. Will you meet up with us before we go out to meet her?"

"Oh. Really. Of course. But why isn't he flying straight out here? Fairbanks is a little out of the way."

"Ennie—I mean *Jacob*—all brothers don't hate each other. Some of us still like to see each other."

"Fine. Yes, I'll see you when you get here. I'll dial Dal now and see if he's on board."

Jake shifted uncomfortably in the metal clutch of an airfield station-gate chair. Outside, three black-and-gray dirigibles floated in the airfield sky, rising and lowering slowly, their tethers trailing down like tentacles. His parka and gear filled the chair beside him. Across the aisle, a cluster of suited Japanese businessmen bantered privately. A hearty young man in plaid wool slapped the back of a bearded Russian in a sable hat. A wiry guy in glasses from the Lower 48, sporting a patched-together attempt at cold-weather wear, whispered into a portable tape recorder.

Jake scowled. He leafed through curling leaves of thermographic fax paper. The phone call transcripts from Jacob had been waiting for him at the post office.

Guess I should read these.

Jacob's tidy, all-caps handwriting graced the top of the page: ALLY: HERE'S THE LATEST FROM DOWN IN TEXAS. The dialog commenced in purple typescript of varying density.

> 2: Shes a pretty sharp cookie. And I found out some more stuff that makes sense.

ONE OF THESE THINGS IS NOT LIKE THE OTHER

1: Okay like what.

2: Are you transcribing now.

1: Of course.

2: Okay so Brett Ashley lived outside New Garton for several months as part of this commune. She gave birth to a boy then left town she shows up back with her family on the east coast no baby no boyfriend got it.

1: Yeah.

2: UNINTELLIGIBLE While Dad is living out in the woods. His wife goes into labor, gives birth to more than one child, and dies. Dad leaves town a few months later.

1: Thats when he moved to Idaho right. Thats where we lived after we were born. Mm listen this is fascinating but were quads remember we all look alike. Were brothers. Dad had 4 sons. This waitress of yours is confused and the rest must just be coincidence.

2: What are you trying to say. That the waitress and Brett are both confused. Well maybe its an accident. Youve heard of doppelgangers right. UNINTELLIGIBLE

1: So what your saying Dad accidentally found an unrelated boy of the same age who looked exactly like the other boys. Thats highly plausible.

2: Well maybe he went down to the commune sometime and had an affair with Brett. That would explain why we look like him. Or then theres plastic surgery.

1: Oh right or maybe he made us all out of clay. Maybe were space aliens. Dallas Dad wouldnt let us near a doctor. We didnt even receive our vaccinations until we lived at the service station. I don't understand why your so certain about this. Why do you want 1 of us to be fake.

2: I dont I just. I want to know the truth. I want to know what to believe in I want I want all this stuff Im finding out to mean something. I dont want 1 of us to be fake. I just want to know the truth and. The truth may be that 1 of us is fake.

1: Look your still coming with us to meet Brett right.
2: Yeah.
1: Will you believe whatever she tells us.
2: Yeah.

The transcript finished in a jagged tear from where his brother had ripped it from the reel. Above the tear, tidy capitals added: WE JUST ARGUED AFTER THIS.

An intercom crackled. "Yukon Airways airship number 501 from Portland, Oregon, now descending at Platform Three."

Jake folded the transcripts into the envelope and stuffed it into his flannel shirt pocket. The disembarking crowd trickled down the walkway.

Jake stood and saw himself—head shaved, beard trimmed into a meticulous stripe down the chin, eyes blued by contact lenses—but nevertheless his own face.

Jake coughed and licked his lips. He nodded. His brother nodded back. They left the airfield station together.

"The snow looks like confetti." His brother nodded toward the windshield of Jake's truck.

"Huh?"

"All swirling around in the headlights. It looks like confetti on New Year's." The highway stretched before them into blue-blackness. Rows of short trees, stunted by the thin air, mobbed the sides of the two-lane road. Snowflakes circled and whirled in the truck's displacement of air.

"Isn't confetti all different colors?" Jake asked. He flexed his fingertips around the steering wheel and glanced over at his brother.

"Yeah. It could be glitter, though. Or white confetti. Like at the White Party."

"What's a white party?"

"It's a circuit party. They're amazing. Gay guys from all over the country go. Like thousands. Everything's white, and everyone dresses all in white until they, ah, well, most of them end up taking their clothes off."

"You go to it?"

"No. But I've been to some like it. You should come down

to one some time."

"I don't think those guys would like me."

"No, no really. Some guys are really into Bears these days. Bears are big, hairy guys like you."

"I'm not somebody's 'Bear.'"

"I'm sorry. I'm just saying it wouldn't hurt you to try to meet somebody."

"Not interested."

"Look, you can play Miss Bachelor with the rest of us, but you know I know better. I worry about you."

Jake glared at his brother in the passenger seat. The well-groomed, well-dressed version of himself. His Hollywood brother. If this really was a movie, Jake would be the real person, and Hollywood would be the actor hired to portray him.

Jake returned to the road ahead. His brother gazed at the black outside the passenger window.

"How far is your place?"

"About an hour."

Twenty silent minutes later, Jake cleared his throat. "Thanks."

"Huh?" His Hollywood brother had dozed off.

"Thanks for taking care of everything at Dad's. I know I could've come down and helped, but I just didn't want to see it all. I couldn't go back there. By the time I would've gotten down there you would've been done already."

"Oh. It's okay. No biggie. I was already down there. You know, you do what's got to be done."

"And thanks for coming out here."

"It's okay."

"None of the rest of us would've done it."

Jake's breath fogged the passenger window. "It's okay."

"It was weird being secret again. Compared to living in West Hollywood."

Jake held the shot glass against his mouth. The whiskey-trickle burned down his throat, fumes rising up his sinuses. He ran his tongue along the lip of glass.

"Huh," he said in a nonplussed half-grunt. "You and the sheriff, huh?" Jake set his shot glass on the steamer trunk between him and his brother, avoiding his eyes.

"After the church bazaar," his brother said, "everyone went toward the park, and I went along with the crowd. I went to go see him play in a benefit softball game." His brother seemed distant and dreamy, gazing up into the rafters of the cabin, idly stroking the furs swaddling him on the couch.

"All the bleachers were full. There wasn't an empty seat except for the ones boxed off for the mayor. When she came, the game started." His brother stretched out, the pelts and military-surplus blankets gathered up to his neck.

"I brought binoculars. He looked so hot in his softball uniform. It said 'Los Toros' on the back. 'The Bulls.' I thought that was funny, a Spanish name for a softball team in Oregon. Turns out the coach was the son of Mexican migrant workers.

"I was sitting in the bleachers up above his team's cages. He didn't look up at me much, but he was always down in front where I could see him, watching, playing catch, stretching. He was so showing off for me.

"His team won. And after the game, he came over, even with everyone around, and I congratulated him on the game. And he hugged me. And he took his ball cap and put it on my head.

"I hate baseball caps, you know? They're just a little too gay, and they just scream of some old fag who's self-conscious about losing his hair. But it was so sweet of him to give it to me. A corny gesture, but sweet, and I just gave in to it. The cap was all sweaty. And it smelled like him. I wore it all the rest of the day." His brother poured himself another shot and knocked it back. Jake watched him silently.

"God, he's hot," his brother moaned. "And the sex was like—like nothing else. I mean, I had no idea."

Sitting in the rocker, Jake shifted his weight, frowning. "I can't believe you did it with him in Dad's house." He drew his arms across his chest.

His brother drew in a slow inhale, breath gliding between his lips while he searched for words. "It felt like, like he cared so much about me. Even when he was talking like a total pig. He said—"

"You know," Jake said, interrupting his brother. He sat up in the rocker and leaned forward. "It'll get cold down here when the fire goes out," he told him. "You'll have to wake up to feed the fire."

His brother nodded, staring into the fireplace, face cocked with a lingering half-smile.

"My stove upstairs in the loft, it lasts longer," Jake pressed. "It keeps warm all night."

"I'm fine down here."

"I just thought it'd be warmer," Jake said. "With me. That's all."

His brother nodded.

Jake reached over, tipping the rocker on edge, and poured himself another shot. He filled his brother's empty glass. The liquor quivered in his unsteady hand. Jake eyed the firelight refracted through whiskey, a dancing, rutilant djinn.

"Well, just have to stock up on liquid fire, then!" he said, forcing merriment. His brother smiled and sat up on the couch. They clinked glasses. They drank. Each exhaled loudly.

Jake's eyes watered. His brother's shaved head wasn't as notable in the deep, shifting shadows. In the umbral firelight, he looked more like him.

Jake pulled the bearskin closer around his legs, creaking the rocker. He had a hard-on. The fire cackled. Jake tasted whiskey on the roof of his mouth. He stared at his brother and pressed his lips together.

"I know why Dad died."

"Yeah, he was crazy. Fucking drama queen. And that video and everything! Control queen, too."

"No, I know why he really died."

"What're you talking about? You weren't even there."

"But I know why he really did it."

"So do I—he was psycho."

"You don't mean that."

"He'd lost it, girl. All those computers? He'd finally gone over the edge. I saw him at the end. He was bitchcakes. You know, crazy."

"I saw him just a couple of months before. He wasn't crazy. You can't be crazy and know how to work all those machines. You can't be crazy and make that video, leave us all those instructions. Yeah—you were there, so tell me this— didn't Dad know exactly what he was doing?"

"Yeah. But you can be crazy and know exactly what you're doing, if what you're doing is the crazy part."

"He wasn't crazy!" Jake slammed his glass down on the

trunk. His face softened. "He was angry. He was punishing us."

"You are so full of shit."

"I started it. Then he did it in front of you. He was punishing us. You and me especially."

"What are you talking about? What did we do?"

"We loved each other. We loved each other more than we loved him."

"What do you mean? We all hate him. But I hate Ennie, too."

"Glowie, it's more than that—"

"Don't start calling me that!" His brother ran his palm over his scalp and sighed. "I'm sorry, just please don't start with that."

Jake lowered his head. "Before your visit—when Dad—"

"Yeah?"

"I was the last one to go out there. I'd been out to visit him not long before."

"You saw a lot of him, huh?"

"Well—more than any of the rest of us."

"So. You were down there in Oregon."

"Yeah. Dad and I never did a whole lot. I'd show up and do some work around there. Last few times or so he'd been all busy with all his machines. I worked on the house or garden, whatever needed tending to."

"Damn, he had a lot of stuff. Packing all that up took forever, even with all the church ladies. Did he ever show you what any of that stuff was all for?"

"No. Said I was too stupid to understand how it worked. He'd shoo me off if I tried watching over his shoulder."

"The hard drive had been cleaned out before he died. I didn't find anything in there beyond the stuff we saw in the will."

"That didn't have anything to do with why he killed himself."

"Oh? Yeah? Then you tell me what it's all about."

Jake stood up and tossed back his liquor. He walked across the small cabin to the windows. He pulled aside the deerskin hanging in front of the frosty glass.

His brother studied him from the couch.

"I haven't seen you in a long time," Jake said from the

window. "You never come see any of us. You hadn't seen Dad in years—"

"Hey, don't start blaming me for what Dad did! He couldn't even tell which of us I was. He thought I'd just been there to visit him before."

"I know—I'm not saying that's why he did it. I'm just saying—I know we're all far away, and I miss all of us, but, you know, you the most sometimes."

His brother waved him off. "You're just lonely," he said. "You wouldn't miss us if you had friends and other people in your life. And you know what would help with that, but I'm not going to have that fight with you again."

"What?" Jake turned from the window.

"You know."

The brothers stared at each other.

"If you'd just admit you're a fag, living your life would be a whole lot easier. And less lonely."

Jake's eyes watered. He stood at the foot of the sofa. His brother swung his feet out across the steamer trunk. Jake sat beside him.

"Here," his brother said. He lifted the quilt and blankets off his legs and draped them across Jake. He stretched and wiggled his sock toes at the wood stove's heat.

"I don't want to preach at you, but how do you expect to ever meet anyone, ever have anyone in your life, if you're still in the closet?"

"I don't need your life," Jake said. "I don't need a whole bunch of sex clubs and men sticking their dicks through the wall in public bathrooms—"

"Hey, gay guys don't all do that stuff all the time. Tearooms and baths are just, like, a good way for men who aren't out yet to meet each other. Guys that are scared— sometimes that's the only way they can start out meeting other guys. I'm sorry. I'm just always trying to let you know how much there is out there you could be taking advantage of. That could help you meet someone. Someone you could have something real with. Like I think I might."

"I don't need all that."

"Then don't bitch to me about being lonely." They stared at the stove's glow. His brother ran his palm across the fuzz of his scalp. "I don't see what all this has to do with him."

Jake pulled on his beard. "It happened when I was visiting. I'd been weeding all afternoon. That night when I came in, Dad was with all his machines. He'd already eaten and didn't want to talk or nothing. So I went upstairs into his loft."

"He let you sleep up there? He made me take the couch."

"He had me sleep up there because he'd work on his machines all night, then just sleep on the couch."

"Yeah, well, he'd just wake me up when he came down and started working on them at dawn." His brother sighed.

Jake rubbed his face, swallowed. "So I would spend nights up there, and I'd start looking at the picture."

"That one I sent you?"

Jake nodded, listening. "You remember," he said, "you remember that day?" He looked at his brother.

"Oh yeah! We'd been swimming instead of clearing rocks and, um, that was when we kept dunking Chairhesty, and Crowking got all pissy, yelling at us to be more mature." He smiled. "We still had fun together then. Until Dad got home at least."

Jake coughed. "I know. I was looking at that picture. We're in the front on the rocks, and the others are in the water. I must've been looking at that picture forever. I forgot about everything else. Forgot about being in Oregon and Dad being downstairs. Felt like it was just like back then and we were all together and—" He looked at his brother. Their eyes glowed with reflected stove-light, brown red embers ready to spark or crack open. "And you and me were together."

His brother narrowed his eyes, frowned. His lips pressed together tightly.

Jake spoke faster. "And I was just thinking about that and looking at the picture, and we're all wet and beautiful, and the water and sun was on everyone's skin. I was just remembering about all of us, and it gets so lonely. Glowie, I wasn't thinking. I got stupid. I—I starting touching myself. I'm so used to being alone and not having anyone else around."

His brother stared at him, hard.

"And then I heard Dad. He'd come upstairs, and I hadn't heard him, but then I did. He was standing right behind me at the top of the stairs, and he saw what I was doing, and he saw what I was looking at and, and—he said, 'That's it.' I turned around, and he was shaking his head, saying, 'That's it. That's it. That's the end of it.'

"He went back downstairs. I thought he was going to come back up and kill me right there, and I halfway wanted him to. But he just went back to his machines all night." He turned to his brother. "Don't you see? 'That's the end of it.' I killed Dad. From seeing what I did. From seeing how I love you. Seeing how I still love you."

His brother jumped off the couch, blankets falling to the floor. He stormed into the dark kitchen, hitting his head on the hanging rack of pans and skillets. Then silent—Jake knew his brother was watching him from the kitchen's blackness.

"Fuck!"

"Glow—"

"Fuck you! Fuck this shit and fuck you! I can't believe I came all the way up here for this shit!" He walked back to the stove, rubbing his head. "This is all just bullshit so you never have to come out or grow up. Damn, what were you thinking? We were always so careful. We even hid it from the rest of us. What happened to you? We used to wait until four in the morning! We used to hike out miles into the woods!"

"I know. I'm sorry."

"So what. So he found out one more of his sons was a fag. He didn't give a shit when I told him. I thought it might make me special somehow or different at least, but no, no big deal. He probably already knew about me. And you. And us. I'm sure he did. So why should he kill himself over any of us?"

"Because it is us, together—"

"It wasn't us together. It was you and a *picture*—"

"But it was enough for him to know. He figured out everything."

"Bullshit! There's nothing to figure out because nothing's going on. That was years ago. We were kids, and it's over. And he probably already knew. You've got to grow up."

Jake chewed on his thumbnail. He leaned forward on the couch, stood up. "He did know. He knew how we loved each other. He knew it was the only way we could be stronger than him. And he knew what would be the only way to stop us, to destroy us."

"What?" His brother turned around, arms tight at his sides and fists clenched. Jake got up off the couch and walked toward him as if approaching an animal, palms open and facing out.

"Easy, easy. Remember what he said in the email. 'Without me you're nothing. You've never appreciated that, but now I will show you.' He thinks he made us and that we'll go to pieces without him."

Jake stood face-to-face with his brother.

"Our love keeps us strong now. And now we know there's nothing wrong with our love. One of us is obviously not Dad's son. We're not brothers—that's why we're in love.

"I do not—"

"And we'll be dead if we don't watch each other's back. The others aren't going to like having a fake. Brett warned me. And they aren't going to like finding out about us." Jake leaned forward. "We need each other to survive this all."

He put his hands on his brother's shoulders and drew him into a kiss. Their hard cocks crossed each other through layers of thermal cotton.

Jake's dogs blinked sleepily, raising their heads at the sound of breaking glass. The men's shouts and swearing ripped across the hissing silence of the night. Some dogs stood up, watching intently, at attention, on the other side of the chain-link fence. They twitched at the sound of furniture overturning, large bodies thudding against the floor of the cabin, wood and glass cracking and breaking.

Some dogs whined at the sound of their master's voice, raging shouts of accusation and defense. That their master's voice was duplicated only confused things more. The sounds of fighting were clear. Pain, anger, and love were apparent in the duplicate voices, but who gave and who received? Who was screaming; who was pleading?

The dogs paced nervously when the noise stopped. They howled, whined, and called out. A hand drew the skins back shut over the broken window and light from the cabin died. The dogs cried, whimpered, paced.

They slept fitfully. Morning came and went. Even though there was no sunlight, the dogs' stomachs told them something was wrong. Their feeding was late. When sounds finally came from the cabin, they bolted to the fence.

Tools and work were supposed to come *after* feeding.

ONE OF THESE THINGS IS NOT LIKE THE OTHER

Some howled, singing in unison with the chainsaw's whine.

When the dogs finally ate, they ate better than they ever had, feasting on fresh meat. Only when sated did they note the kennel's open gate. It swung freely. The pack left the kennel together.

NEW YORK

"Well, our West Coast brethren just couldn't find time to join us, it seems," Jacob explained. "But I'm calling from New York, and Dal, where the hell are you, Dal?"

Jacob stood over his tiny, three-burner stove, watching the water boil in a dented aluminum saucepan. He reached around the hanging baskets of potatoes, onions, and garlic to grab a squeezy bear of honey from the overcrowded shelves.

His brother cleared his throat. "I'm just in Oklahoma. Actually, I'm right near where they shot off that gun and had the land rush."

"Really, now?" said the waitress from New Garton.

"Fascinating, Dal," Jacob said.

"Yeah, but I'll be driving all through today and tonight to get out east, Enwycie. You get the name of my motel I sent you?"

"Jacob. Yes, and why the hell did you pick that place? It's not even near Gravesend." Jacob held the squeezy bear upside down over a mug on top of his neurology textbook. He dribbled honey into the mug, golden ropes oozing across the dry sachet of chamomile tea. He always put the honey in first, so the turbulence of pouring in boiling water would help dissolve it.

"Because my friend here from New Garton has friends there who are getting me a good bargain."

"Ah yes, I'm sorry, I was neglecting our guest of honor. Ma'am, I'm transcribing our conversation today, and I'll send carbons to our other two brothers since they can't make this call. I apologize for them."

ONE OF THESE THINGS IS NOT LIKE THE OTHER

"Well, all right, then...Jacob," said the waitress from Texas.

Jacob set the honeybear on top of the dishes in his sink. Frowning, he crooked the phone under his neck and licked the honey-stick from the side of his hand.

"So, if I may sum up what you've told us so far," Jacob said, "You knew Jake—Senior. And that he kidnapped the child of some counterculture girl who you had midwifed." Jacob turned the fire off underneath the saucepan. "But you didn't tell the police what you knew, because you wanted to protect your illegal operation. Your illegitimate career was more important than the kidnapping of an infant boy and murder of his father?"

Dallas leapt to her defense: "Now don't be judging her on—"

"No, it's all right," she said. "Everything looks clear behind you, don't it?"

Jacob tilted the saucepan, carefully pouring water into his mug.

"You got to be more polite, Ennie," Dal instructed. "This lady's been helping us a lot, and she saved my life with the snake business and all."

"Oh, all right," Jacob snapped. "I'm just trying to understand." The phone cord stretched taut as Jacob leaned back against the plastic shower shell. He blew on his tea to cool it.

"I'll warn you, though," she said. "You boys might understand, but that don't mean you'll believe."

"Try me," sighed Jacob.

"Ennie—!" Dal growled in exasperation.

"Oh all right, all right. I'll be quiet."

The waitress cleared her throat. "First off," she said, her voice steady and controlled, "your father was very proud of having four boys, and you all know that better than me. I think that baby in your mother's grave was one of his original four, and he died, and he was replaced by the hippie girl, this Brett woman, by her child. No one would've been on the serious hunt for a missing bastard whose mother wouldn't even claim him. *And* if he looked just like his 'brothers,' no one would question that they weren't all family. *And* as they got older, and looked more and more like the spitting image of Jake Senior, no one would question that they weren't his."

Jacob bit his lower lip, fingers drumming a stack of textbooks on top of his fridge. "Exactly," he said. "Which is why your story makes no sense."

"So let me tell you another story," she said quietly. "I am sorry I didn't tell you this right away, Jake, but I didn't want you to think I was some crazy old broad. I was trying to nudge you in the right direction, get you to keep checking this out. I'm glad you're going to Gravesend now. But, at the time, I know you wouldn't've believed, and you might've not come this far. I wanted to help you, well, fulfill your destiny by going back to New England, back to your mother.

"That's perfectly all right," Dallas said.

"All right, I'll tell you my truth. Nothing makes much sense, but the truth rarely does."

Jacob looked through the tiny window next to his shower at his view of airshaft bricks. The waitress began her story.

"After the sheriff had gone there, I went out to Jake's place to check on those boys. Jake was suspicious of me, but he knew he needed help, and I said I just was bringing him some homemade applesauce for them.

"Now, yes, Jake had four babies. Boys. I was suspicious, just because quads are so rare, and I knew Brett's baby had been kidnapped. That's just too much excitement at one time for a town this small for it not to be connected. But none of Jake's babies looked like the one I'd helped deliver for Brett. Brett's baby had been born with pretty blond hair. His father looked Swedish or something. Jake's boys had curly red hair. They were all bigger than the baby I'd midwifed. Different expressions, too.

"I was looking at them, looking for some clue. They were in perfect health, and I told Jake so, and told him how sorry I was about his losing his wife. He didn't have much to say, just glared at me.

"Then something happened I couldn't explain. I saw a flicker out of the corner of my eye, from where the baby in the furthest corner of the crib was. I looked over at him, and I swear I saw him change. His hair especially, it flickered like the last gasp of light when you turn off a TV, except it flickered yellow. The red flickered pale blond, then was red again.

"Jake told me I had to leave. I tried to stall, saying how impressed I was he'd delivered the boys, that'd I never even seen quads before. He was steering me to the door and—I couldn't help myself, I've always been kind of mouthy—I said I didn't realize that they could have different colored hair.

"That night I was at home. We'd just had supper, and the phone rang. He didn't say who he was. He just said, if I told anyone, he'd take *my* little boy away from me."

"He'd kidnap your son?" asked Jacob.

"No. He'd take him. My boy wouldn't be mine any more. Then he hung up."

Jacob persisted. "What do you mean?" Closing his eyes and rubbing his temple, he leaned backward and nearly fell into his shower. He grabbed the brittle siding, nails scraping against the cracked plastic.

"I didn't know right then, but I was scared enough not to tell my husband. That night our boy woke me up crying. He wasn't crying like normal. He was wailing, howling. I ran into his room. He was tossing around in his bed, and I grabbed him and held him. He started coughing and wheezing, then got silent. I turned him around to see if he was okay. He looked up at me, smiling, but with your father's face.

"I wanted to scream but didn't want to scare him more. All the sudden his face wrinkled up, and he looked normal again. He asked me what Mommy was doing in his bedroom, why I'd woken him up. Then I thought for sure I was going crazy, that your father had scared me into going crazy, having these dreams."

Jacob took a deep drink of his tea. He realized his hand was clenching the mug. He let go, stretching and flexing his sore fingers.

"But then the phone rang. I just froze and let my husband answer it. My son and I just sat there, staring at each other. I heard my husband say, 'What?' and 'No,' and grumble and hang up. My son and I kept staring at each other. Then he crawled under the covers, just his eyes peeking out at me. I asked if he was okay, if he could get to sleep. He nodded his head. I went back to the bedroom.

"My husband asked how our son was. I said fine, just a nightmare. I asked him who was on the phone, and he said it was a hang-up.

"The sheriff questioned everyone in town about the hippie boy murder. But he never found out about the child. Brett didn't tell anyone about her baby boy. She was scared quiet after what your father did to her boyfriend. My husband kept quiet about delivering her baby. He wanted to protect us. He didn't know how much he was. I never said a word about their kid, either. And I never told anyone about what I'd seen Jake do. I kept a lot of secrets, living in this town, but that was the only secret I ever kept from my husband."

Jacob cleared his throat. He closed his wet eyes, rolling them back in his head. He scratched his chin. "You guys, this is just getting more and more insane. Dal, I think you've gone crazy from the dust down there. This is crazy, right?"

"I said y'all wouldn't believe it," she said.

"Listen," said his brother. "I know these pieces of the story are incredible, but they fit together. They make sense."

"I just don't know what to say," Jacob muttered. "Dal, I can't believe you're being such a schmuck, just sitting there listening to all this."

"Look," he pleaded, "just think it over. See how it feels to you. How it feels like the way we feel. That's what's convincing me. This *feels* right. This feels like my memory of Mom."

"Let's just see Brett. Will that put an end to this? Will that clean this all up, fix things for you? I can't argue anymore. I've got to get to my shift."

"Excuse me," the waitress said, "I've said enough for now. I'll let y'all hash this out." She hung up.

"I'll send a transcript of this call to Hollywood and Alaska on my way to the hospital," Jacob said. "But they may not get it—they're due in here early tomorrow." He made an exasperated "phht!" sound. *I'm really sick of all this.*

Jacob hung up. Shaking, he turned into his kitchen's shower and started water flowing. He stuck his head under the spray, turning left to right with his mouth open, sucking the dribbles into his mouth.

Early the next morning, Jacob bolted up from bed. He tossed off his comforter and stepped into slippers on the floor. He walked with the proficiency of the blind through his dark apartment to the phone. His finger circled the dial, calling his brother's motel outside town.

"Did you have the dream?"

"What? What are you talking about?"

"Did you just have a dream about us? One of us?"

"Man, it was a real long drive here from Texas. I've been asleep."

"How could you not feel this? It was intense, like the old days. God, it feels like he's right here in the room with me."

"Calm down, it's just all of us coming to town, that's all. Why don't you catch your breath for a sec and tell me what all you dreamed."

A long, slow breath escaped from Jacob. "I'm fine. But I think something happened to Holly or Ally." Jacob ran his hand through his hair. "So you didn't feel anything?" He scowled.

"No. What did you feel?"

"I just felt one of them—it's funny I couldn't tell which—and—something wrong. That's about all I can say."

"Like an airship implosion?"

"I don't know."

"Well, turn on the TV," his brother sighed. Jacob spun around the TV on top of the fridge to face him and clicked it on.

"If there's been an implosion, the networks'll be humping it for all it's worth. What's on?"

Jacob turned the dial, changing channels. "It's just the early-morning news," he muttered.

"Anything about an implosion?"

Jacob wiped the sweat from his forehead. On the TV, the chipper hosts nibbled pink and purple edible teacups.

"No," Jacob muttered.

"Look, I didn't feel a thing, so I think this was just a nightmare of yours."

"You didn't feel anything?"

"Nope."

Silence. Jacob circled the inside of his mouth with his tongue. He pressed the fingers of his free hand against his temple.

"Look," his brother said. "I think this whole thing is getting under our skin. I think we need to see Brett as soon as possible."

"How are you so certain she's your mother?"

His brother sighed in frustration. "I didn't say that! Look, Holly and Ally get here later. Pick them up, stop by my motel, then we'll all head out to Gravesend together, right?"

"Okay." Jacob nodded slowly in the dark. He pursed

his lips.

"Now get some sleep."

Jacob hung up. He fished around in the hanging wire baskets above the toilet for his antianxiety meds, opened the bottle, and dumped two into his palm. He glanced at the news show's time: 5:42. Jacob groaned, slid one pill back into the bottle and took the other. He stepped out of his kitchen and threw himself onto his bed.

Looking up, he realized the TV was still turned away from him toward the phone. "Fuck," he sighed. The news show's plucky banter and flashing lights filled the kitchen. The dim blue glow of predawn hovered outside the airshaft window. Jacob pulled the pillow over his head.

Grandkids ruin everything. Disregard that trifle concerning how everyone loves being a grandpa, eh? Everyone spoils their grandkids. And it's the grandkids who spoil everything. That's why I put a stop to it. They undermine the parental authority. First they make the parent act like a buffoon. They reveal the parent's hypocrisy and soft spot. When grandkids are born, the children see their parents and their acts in a whole new light, and I don't aim to fall into that hole. I won't be axed by them. I said aloud it's not allowed. I won't be knocked from my berth by grandkids' birth.

Now also the grandkids teach their parents something. They give the parents that unconditional love. When the kids start receiving that, it alters their whole world. You are usurped from your altar. Coup d'état. Because until then, even though kids never fully return the love to their father, they are wont to care. They do want something. They don't want to give him anything; they want to wrest away. They won't rest until getting his approval. And that's the standoff.

The father always wants the love and never gets it; the sons always want the approval and never get it. That's the balance; that's the harmony. From there the symphony blossoms. Grandkids affect the discordant chord, and I have no interest in modernism. I cut the extension cord, because when the sons receive that love, feel that heir-love in the air for their own sons, they no longer care about approval from their father. I won't allow that effect. That's why I had you boys all fixed. Yes, pumpkin, you didn't acquire that insight, did you? No accident to incite your sterility, no company chemicals as in that story of yore. You're mine and I'm yours. You might have girlfriends and the like. If not a Mary, you might even marry, but it won't be merry. I'm too in you, and you're too in each other. It's too much for any woman to stand for long. You'll always come back to me, back to each other, back to us.

Jacob opened his eyes, sighed. He swung his legs over the side of the bed. Pale, icy light illuminated his apartment. He blinked and rubbed his forehead. He stared at the floor, his father's dream lingering in his mind.

Jacob shook his head clear and reached for his journal on the nightstand. He knocked over a glass of water and the bottle of aspirin from the night before.

"Fuck!" he hissed, mopping the spill with the corner of his blanket. The cheap pink acrylic did little to absorb the water but did manage to pick up a good amount of lint, hairs, and unclassifiable grime from the floor.

Grimacing, Jacob rearranged the blanket to avoid the wet, dirty corner. He propped up his pillow and unclipped the pen from the side of his diary.

> Another fucking Dad dream—can't remember it exactly—all this dreck about how grandchildren are evil.
>
> Woke up earlier with a bad feeling about Holly—called Dallas at his motel here, and he said he didn't feel a thing. It was intense—there's either something wrong with him—I can't believe he didn't feel it! Or I'm feeling things now that aren't real—I'm going crazy.
>
> I have to remind myself there is a difference between craziness and family.
>
> Or not. Dad goes and our union falls apart. All run to this woman for help, for answers. I don't know why I'm going along with this. The only answer is yourself. <u>You can only help yourself.</u>
>
> Still—I'm sickly curious about what she knows. What if she is my mother? Why did I gravitate to this part of the country? Why did I never fit in with my brothers? Do I even want another parent? Can she heal everything Dad did, or will she just take over screwing with our lives?
>
> I'm so sick of all this—I just want everyone to

leave me alone, let me get on with my life. I had to take double shifts next week to clear today for this damn reunion. Fuck, I just wish this was all over. I wish I was alone in my city again, working and studying. Preparing for converting, completing my internship. Living my own life.

A normal life, with a house someday, not this shoebox. And a cat. Cats. Like at the service station. She had a whole brood of cats that were practically wild but loved her completely. They roamed the tall brown weeds behind the station and slunk in and out of the rusted buggy frames. I remember them scratching their claws on the rotting wood sideboards of that old station wagon.

She named all of them but couldn't always remember all of them. She'd get confused after a couple dozen names, then she'd go outside and spy some she'd forgotten: "Oh, and there's Big Daddy Dirtbag!" She'd have her skirt pulled up against the grass and metal skeletons of cars, with the cats circling her feet, looking up at the lace hem of her dress, their crafty yellow eyes contemplating a pounce.

She'd just say, "Oh, and there's Poopie! So Sloopie must be around here somewhere!"

It makes me smile to remember. I sort of want to be like her some day, somehow. Settle down. Be a dotty old guy with a bunch of cats—although I'm not naming them 'Poopie.' Happy, just lost in my world, unconscious of being any different and not having to try so hard to be different OR normal.

Jacob closed his diary and tossed it onto the blanket next to him. Diffuse gray light illuminated the bricks across from his window. He stared glumly at nothing. The city clanked, yelled, and rumbled outside.

Jacob shut the door to his tenement building. He tested the handle to make sure it was locked. He looked up and down the avenue, blinking in the morning's slanted yellow light. He inhaled: raw flesh's sweet scent drifted from the building down the block where men butchered suspect meat for street carts. He braced his shoulders and strode decisively in the opposite direction, around the block.

Jacob pulled his hand from his pants pocket. He held open the market door for an exiting Russian woman, her head wrapped in a navy wool scarf. She bustled past him and down the street without comment. He stepped into the market, the bell on the door jangling as it shut behind him. The store smelled of musty, old paper and ripe produce. A fly buzzed past him.

Jacob wedged down the narrow aisle to the produce racks. He looked dubiously at bruised mangoes and overripe bananas.

Maybe it'll have to be the donut shop after all this morning.

Jacob brightened upon noticing the storekeeper's nine-year-old son stacking yams beside him.

"Hey buddy!"

The boy smiled. "Hi, Jake!"

"That's Jacob."

"Yeah, hi, Jake!"

"Yeah..." Jacob squatted to face the boy. He grabbed a tomatillo and rolled it over in his palm. It looked like a cross between a garlic and a green tomato; his thumb picked at the gray green outer paper until he could rub the shiny green skin underneath. "Say, you know what these are for?" He held the tomatillo up to the boy's face.

"It's a tomatillo," he said authoritatively.

Jacob nodded and smiled. "Do you eat them?"

The boy shrugged. "*Some*body does, I guess."

Jacob nodded sagely. "Do you know where they come from?"

"From the truck," he explained patiently.

"Yeah," Jacob said, "but where does the truck get them? What are they?"

"*I* don't know."

Jacob smiled and clasped the boy on the shoulder. "They're rats' eggs!" he explained brightly. "From Hawaii. Giant Hawaiian rats come crawling out of them at night when they hatch."

"Ma!" the boy shouted, eyes wide.

Jacob stood up and looked down the aisle. The storekeeper

waved merrily at him. "Hello, Mr. Barnes, how are you this morning?"

"Fine, fine. And you?" Jacob smiled back at her.

"Oh, very good," she said. She nodded at the tomatillo in Jacob's hand. "You like those?"

Jacob shot the boy a wry glance. "I don't know. What you do with them?"

"Mexican fruit," she said, nodding. "You make special sauce." Her son groaned loudly and punched Jacob in the leg.

Grinning, Jacob eyed the fruit. "Are they sweet?"

She pursed her lips. "Oh, no," she said, turning to a new customer but waving her hand in the air toward Jacob. "No, no, not sweet. Sour!" She nodded across the counter at the man in the green hoodie.

"Giant rats," the boy muttered.

Jacob nodded and put the tomatillo back. He peered bemusedly at a jicama. He heard the shopkeeper's gasp.

"Mrs.—" He turned around to see the new customer pointing his hoodie pocket at her, apparently with a gun inside.

"Ma!" her son shouted. The man turned toward Jacob and the boy.

"Get down!" Jacob hissed. The boy took a step toward the counter but Jacob lunged for him. He grabbed the boy's waist and fell to the dusty floor on top of him, knocking over a mound of grapefruit, which bounced merrily down the aisle.

"What the fuck?" shouted the thief.

Jacob pulled the squirming boy tight to his chest and dragged him back behind the aisle divider. "We've got to hide back here," he whispered to the boy. "And stay quiet!" He laid his palm over the boy's mouth and held him protectively, stroking his hair.

"Here, here," he could hear the shopkeeper say to the thief. "Here. I got money."

"Right—the money! Give it to me, lady!"

Jacob listened until he heard the door jangle closed. He peered around the aisle. "Is he gone?" he called out.

She nodded and stumbled down the aisle toward them. "Ma!" her son cried as Jacob helped him up. He ran to his mother, and Jacob looked her over quickly to make sure she wasn't hurt.

"I'm okay," she said as she grabbed her snuffling son.

"And I gave him only a little money."

"I'll call the police," Jacob said, moving up to the counter. "You two—" He looked back at the mother and son comforting each other. "Take care of each other." *That's what mothers are for, isn't it?*

Why the hell did those two have to fly in to the farthest possible airfield station? Jacob groaned in relief upon pushing open the door with the blue circle and arrow.

Jacob took the furthest stall. He yanked down his pants and sat on the toilet, preparing to release.

The stall next to him opened and closed. The door latched. "Fuck," Jacob grumbled. No pee came. Jacob tried not to think about the person next to him. He tried to breathe slowly and relax his abdomen, but an increasingly strong feeling impelled him to turn and look to his left.

He looked over at the seat-cover dispenser. The paper seats had been all pulled out and the cardboard back of the container ripped out. There was nothing behind it. No steel wall or metal plate—it was a hole into the adjoining stall. "Fuck," Jacob whispered. He leaned back and stared straight ahead at his stall door. He closed his eyes and imagined running water: a river; a creek; the creek behind their house from that photo Holly had sent—

Paper rustled next door. Jacob turned and looked at the stall divider. The hole in the wall was now full. A thick, pink penis jutted through the hole into his stall, erect and engorged, surrounded by a fiery ring of orange pubic curls and wispy, yellow hairs hanging off the balls. The owner flexed his muscles, making it bob.

"Hey!" Jacob growled. He smacked the cock, as if swatting a fly or the nose of an irksome dog. The penis withdrew, but not entirely.

"Back off before I cut it off," Jacob called out. "You do *not* want to fuck with me today."

The penis withdrew. Jacob sighed. Finally the pee flowed.

"Do I hate airfield stations," Jacob said with exasperation, nodding to his new neighbor. "All the crowds and security are bad enough, but now the people I'm supposed to pick up weren't even on their flight. I'm sure they were running late and missed their flight. That would be so like them. But do they leave me a message at home? Would it kill them to call and let me know what flight they did make? Oh no, they just expect me to sit and wait for them."

His companion in the lounge raised his drink for a toast. "Here's to the things we do for family!"

Jacob smiled. "How'd you know I was here for family?"

"Who else puts us through things like this? My mother bought me this ticket to see her down in Charlotte, but of course it's an itinerary with interminably long layovers and a good half-dozen connections."

"What can you do?" Jacob shrugged.

"I hate flying anyway," he said. "Not for all the little annoyances, and there's plenty of those, but what really chafes me is how an airfield station is such an oxymoronic contradiction. You're going somewhere, you're *traveling*, right? You're in motion. But you spend most of your time at airfield stations waiting. Standing still, sitting, sleeping. Getting somewhere by doing nothing. The illogic of it is frustrating. Especially with short domestic travel. You spend an hour getting outside the city to the airfield station, another two hours checking in, dealing with security, and waiting for the flight and, then, a half hour on the airfield, all for only an hour in the air, then add another hour getting your bags and getting home from the station? That's four-and-a-half hours around an hour of flight, five-and-a-half hours total for cities I could've driven between in less time! That's progress. Thank you Mr. Zeppelin."

Jacob nodded with consternation. "So there." He raised his excessively garnished cocktail to his neighbor and took a deep swig.

"I despise the floor coverings," his companion confided. "The carpeting they use, especially around the gates. It's always these horrid, manic repeating patterns. Such eyestrain gives me a migraine. They're supposed to hide dirt so they don't have to clean so much."

"Headaches." Jacob shook his head. "All the fumes from the cleaners and fuels and disinfectants don't help, either."

His buddy nodded, licking beer foam from his lips. "Yes, certainly. And let's not forget the so-called food."

"Or the prices they charge for it!"

ONE OF THESE THINGS IS NOT LIKE THE OTHER

"Do you know which airfield station offers up surprisingly savory eats? Houston Hobby. Not Intercontinental, Hobby. Shabby airfield station but scrumptious food."

Jacob grimaced at a cart whirring past the bar, lights flashing.

His buddy groaned. "Oh yes. Ceaselessly sneaking up behind you. Flashing lights. Whoop-whoop-whoop! All yield to the geriatrics! Hmpf. Yes. I *also* particularly detest that luggage all the flight crews carry, the ones with the long handles? Always pulling them along with the most assuming air, as if strolling their Afghans on Park Avenue. *Despise* those."

"Yeah?"

"Virulently."

"I hate when people feel the need for fifteen carry-on bags, and the crews never say anything about it to them."

"Mm-hmm." His friend scowled and picked a bit of fluff from his red turtleneck.

"Same people always argue forever at the ticket counter. Must be too stupid to make reservations beforehand."

Jacob's friend tapped his finger thoughtfully on the rim of his beer mug. "You know what else really raises the fur on the back of my neck?" he said. "Fairies! I know they are supposed to be amusing, and one should be tolerant, but sometimes I just want to smack them."

Jacob set down his drink loudly. "Yeah! I had one come on to me in the john here!" He rolled his eyes and bit into a pineapple wedge skewered on a turquoise mermaid's tail.

"There you are." His buddy shook his head. "Pray tell me *why* there are always so many Oscar Wildes at airfield stations? You encounter more of them at these places than anywhere else outside of their own watering holes. Do they possess greater wanderlust than the rest of us? You'd think they'd all be off on cruise ships, or playing cowboys or something. Yet you come to an airfield station, in any locale, and there's simply an inordinate percentage of them scuttling about. Big fairies, little fairies, muscle fairies, furry fairies. They're always the goosey ones, fidgeting unnecessarily. If you catch eyes with them, they look away. As most gentlemen do. However, you know they're fairies if they turn back around and look at *you* to see if you're still looking at *them*. And, if you are, fairies don't get incensed. Their eyes grow immense and sanguine. And often they'll favor you with a shit-eating grin."

Jacob grinned sourly.

His buddy chortled as he polished his large, square tortoiseshell glasses. "Oh dear, I do not want to know about *that*. They're just constantly looking around."

He shook his head and pointed his glasses in different directions as he spoke. "Looking at you, looking at other fairies, looking at themselves. Pray tell what are they looking so hard for? Do they seek out one another for water-closet rendezvous? Hatch plans to join the secret Homo Mile-High Club? Get the dossier on sissy haunts at their next destination?" He reset his glasses indignantly.

"Don't I know!" Jacob exclaimed. "Why does everything still have to be so secret for them? Do they get off on it or something? I mean, times have changed. They have more venues than anonymous sex in bathroom stalls, so why do they still do it? Especially when they're just outside a city with one of the largest gay populations in the world?"

"The allure of the unknown, the forbidden. I think it gets instilled in them at an early age, as part of their psychological makeup, and they keep returning to it. It has to be secret and forbidden to turn them on."

Jacob ate a cherry. "You know what's ironic is, I have a gay brother."

"Oh, I say—" the man held up his palms. "I didn't intend any offense." Coolly he smoothed his thin, gray-and-yellow hair.

Jacob held up his palm. "It's all right. He's a nice enough guy, but I don't need to know all about it. I don't ask him about it, and he doesn't feed me details or anything."

The man nodded emphatically. "Oh, yes, I know, they're swell fellows. I work with them on a daily basis. I'm a buyer for a department-store chain, and in retail you have plenty of them. Half the buyers and almost all of advertising. Charming fellows. I just wonder how they get so much time off to travel?"

"That's who I'm supposed to be picking up. Him and one of my other brothers." Jacob drained his seahorse-shaped glass and checked the time on his pager.

"Ah-ha! Then I believe you are encountering what they refer to as 'Gay Standard Time.'"

"Yes. You know what's the strange part?"

"What's that?"

Jacob leaned into the bar and watched for the bartender's eye. His buddy waited, expectant. Jacob jerked his head when the bartender looked his way. Jacob frowned, pointed at his and his buddy's empty glasses. The bartender nodded. Jacob gave him a perfunctory smile and turned conspiratorially to his buddy. His buddy smiled, licking his lips.

"We're identical. Me and my gay brother."

"You mean like twins?"

"Yeah, we look completely alike. Less so much now—he shaves his head and wears contacts to make his eyes blue. But growing up we looked alike, with the same clothes and hair."

"I say. Did people ever mistake you two? Ever get kissed by any of his paramours?" He chuckled.

"We left home pretty young, so he didn't have boyfriends or anything before then—that I knew about. We live in different cities now."

"Must have been uncanny growing up. You know how boys are, particularly brothers. Salacious talk, boasting and braggadocio, and incessant masturbation. Did he know he was effervescent then? Did he tell you?"

"Nah. I should've known, but somehow I missed it. I guess, like you said, they've got a talent for secrets. Plus we were kind of sheltered and, you know, all scared of sex."

"Yes, well, who isn't?"

They clinked drinks.

"So you never apprehended him, ah, you know, eyeing you peculiarly in the shower?"

Jacob cleared his throat. "Uh, no."

"Do you think he thought about it, though?"

"I never considered it before."

Jacob's buddy raised an eyebrow meaningfully and took a deep drink.

"America Airships Number 652 now descending at platform G7."

Jacob leaned into the shell of the pay phone, plugging one ear to better hear his email–reading service. The service announced solicitations for medical seminars and Middle East travel. "Trash. Trash."

"Subject: none given. Sender: 'Sheriff@clackamas.gov.'"

"Read."

"Message: 'I am the Sheriff of Clackamas County in Oregon, where your father died recently. I was with your brother who was out here handling things, but I need to speak to the rest of you as soon as possible. This is urgent. Please contact me by responding directly to this email. Please do not forward it to your brothers. I need to talk to each of you individually first.' End of Message. Reply? Delete? Save? Forward?"

Jake scowled. "Reply: What is this all about? I have been waiting for him to arrive at the airfield station here. Reply to this message or call my home number in this signature. Close message. Send. Return to new messages."

"From 'Public Station.' Subject: 'Jacob.' Message: 'Jacob: Never mind getting us at the airport. Don't have time to go get Ally. Bitchkate will just have to deal with things for himself. I can't take care of him. I'm writing this from a mall, so don't reply. Just go to Dal's motel, and I'll meet you there. Then we can all go out to Gravesend.' End of Message. Reply? Delete? Save? Forward?"

"'Bitchkate'?" Jacob said.

"I do not understand that command."

Jacob wedged his economy car into a tiny parking space. *Dal, fuck you and your 'bargains.'* He slammed his door and exited. Walking briskly across the motel's parking lot, he passed the adjacent family restaurant and looked over his shoulder. At the base of a white metal stairwell that criss-crossed the end of the three-floor motel, he stopped, looked around, and changed direction. He marched back across the parking lot and into the coffee shop, maneuvering past the families in line at the checkout counter.

"There's a wait, Mister. Just a few minutes."

"Can I just get a latte to go?"

"Sure, I've got nothing else to do," she snapped.

"What flavors do you have?"

She looked over her bifocals at Jacob. "I got strawberry, chocolate, and banana syrups for the milkshakes."

"Oh! I'll try banana. Thanks."

She returned with the cup. Jacob handed her money. He asked for napkins to hold the hot cup.

Jacob rapidly recrossed the parking lot, elbows tucked in close and knees bent slightly so as not to spill the banana latte. He waddled to the stairs and climbed them with large, careful steps. He zigged and zagged down the hallways until he found his brother's room. He kicked his toe against the door and sipped his latte.

The door opened to his Texan mirror. The brothers stared at each other. Slicked-back black hair and glasses faced a red crewcut and mustache. His brother's flannel plaid shirt was unbuttoned, hanging down around a red waffled undershirt with buttons at the neck. His blue jeans were faded and rumpled. Jacob wore a thick, roll-neck black sweater and pale gray chinos; his brother was a jumble of colors and textures. His brother's green eyes had more of a sparkle, and he seemed to be getting more sleep than Jacob, whose pale skin faded to plum underneath his eyes.

"Well now," his brother said, running his hand over his head. "You're early. Come on in."

Jacob nodded and sipped his latte. "Have you heard anything?"

"From who?"

"Holly. Any of us."

"I went back to sleep after you called so early. Then I got up and got some breakfast. Phone hasn't rung, and no one's left me any messages. Next question." His brother grinned.

Jacob sighed irritably. He frowned and drank his latte. "They weren't at the airfield station. Then I got an email from Holly saying he wasn't picking up Ally after all, that he was driving out and would just meet us here at your motel. Which, I might add, could not be any more inconveniently located."

His brother shrugged.

"But I swear there's something wrong," Jacob said, licking his lips. "It's not just the dream. That would've faded by now. Don't you feel it?"

"Sorry," his brother said. "Feelings haven't been very reliable since Dad passed."

Jacob narrowed his eyes. "That first week or so I felt kind of alone. But I think I was just overwhelmed by everything, working through the shock and grief. But now I'm paranoid, I guess. It feels sometimes like one of you is following me. It's driving me crazy. We all went our separate ways to get away from stuff like this."

His brother put a hand on Jacob's shoulder. "Look, man, there's still a lot of crazy business going on. We're getting ready to go see our mother. Have you really thought about that?"

"*Your* mother. *My* mother. Ally's. Holly's. We don't know," he sighed, looking outside at the turnpike.

Jacob collapsed into the cold vinyl chair beside the window. He reached for the phone on the side table. "Dal, you haven't even answered your messages."

He picked up the half-empty bottle of tequila blocking his reach. "Nice," he said sarcastically. He gave his brother a pointed look as he set the bottle back down.

Jake rolled his eyes. "Gimme your coffee," he said, grabbing the cup.

"It's a latte."

His brother shrugged and walked into the bathroom. Jacob lifted up the handset. His finger whipped around the dial in a quick circle.

"Goddamn!" his brother said from the bathroom, spitting into the sink and setting the drink on the counter. "What the hell flavor is that?"

Jacob smirked and cleared his throat. "Room 432." He dialed again, again. He listened.

His brother sauntered back into the room, zipping up.

Jacob put his hand over the mouthpiece and turned to his brother, who was already handing him a pen and notepad. He grabbed the souvenir pen and stationery and wrote.

Thanks, Jacob mouthed. He wrote.

He scowled and looked at his brother. His brother sat on the bed beside Jacob. Jacob looked over at him and something passed between them, an invisible, inaudible shock. His brother frowned and stood up, backing away. He walked to the mirror above the TV and stared at himself.

Jacob hung up the phone. He looked at his brother's reflection, his face aghast. "He's dead."

"What?!"

"Ally's been killed. One of us is dead."

"How the hell—how can that be?"

"The sheriff left a message here. The sheriff in Oregon who handled Dad. Somehow he found out and was trying to contact all of us. I got an email earlier from him, but he didn't say what it was about. This time he did."

"About Ally being dead?"

"That's what they said. A struggle at the cabin, things broken and—" He looked up weakly.

His brother turned from the mirror, shaking his head in shock and staring at the floor. "I can't believe someone would kill Ally."

Jacob advanced toward his brother. "You didn't seem to care before."

Dal's brow furrowed quizzically. "What do you mean before? We just found out."

"I already knew. I felt it. You didn't."

The brothers faced each other.

Jacob's eyes narrowed. "Ally was killed. I felt it. You didn't. And you're the one that was so excited about Brett from the beginning. You took the initiative to go to New Garton and try to prove things. I didn't feel a thing for her. And you have that memory! You said you remember your mother holding you. None of us remember that."

He stepped in closer to his brother, their freckled noses almost touching. "You're Brett's son. You're the fake. It's all true."

His brother ran his fingers through his hair. "Shit, I don't know. We don't all have to be in perfect sync anymore, man. We've been apart for years now. Maybe I am. I don't know."

"Everything is falling apart, and it's all because of you! There's only three of us left—no, only two, because you're not one of us!" Jacob shoved his brother in disgust.

"I don't know what happened to Ally, but it has nothing to do with me. Don't go taking everything out on everyone else like you always do."

"What the fuck are you talking about? One of us is dead, and you're bringing up all this old shit?" His brother glared at him, leaning closer.

Indignant, Jacob shoved him again. His brother's eyes flared wide, and his lips pressed together, blanching. He breathed in deep. He opened his mouth, but no words came out. A loud growl finally broke through, and his fist flew.

Jacob shrieked and jumped onto the bed. His brother turned and tried to grab him, but Jacob bounced across the mattress, stomping on maps spread across the foot of the bed. Jacob leapt onto the floor and glared at his brother with a haughty look of triumph. He raised his hand, but his brother stepped forward and slapped it aside.

Jacob backed into the bathroom. His hands hovered uncertainly in midair. "You just want to ruin everything for all of us," he panted.

"Goddamn you—" his brother wheezed and took a swipe at Jacob, knocking off his glasses. Jacob flinched, jerking back against the bathroom counter and knocking the latte onto the tile floor.

"Why the fuck won't you ever just—be nice to me?" his brother cried out, his face red, eyes tearing up. He stretched out his arms for what could be an attack or an embrace. He threw himself toward Jacob, who jumped out of the way into the bathtub. His brother's foot landed squarely in the spilt latte. He slipped and fell backward, his head slamming against the bathroom-door handle. He bounced off the door and fell, crashing against the side of the bathtub, crumpling onto the floor.

The smell of their sweat filled the room. Jacob saw sparkles swirl through the air as his world faded.

That's my boy!

Jacob opened his eyes, gasped. His knees were against his chest in a fetal position. His mouth opened and lips curled back as if trying to scream. His jaw rolled; his tongue curled silently. His gasps slowed into panting. He rubbed his forehead, rolled over, and sat up. He felt around the bathroom floor for his glasses and put them on.

His brother: next to him, on the floor, facedown. Head bent at an unnatural angle, face pressed into the bathroom tiles at the side of the bathtub. Blood matted the short hairs of his scalp. Jacob looked down at the motionless body, then up at his reflection in the vanity mirror.

Jacob stood, stepped over the body. His breath rushed in and out, hissing past his lips. He blinked, swallowed.

"Stay together," he said in a clear, decisive tone. "Stay together."

He slapped his cheeks rapidly six times. Washed his face. He pulled off his sweater and took it into the bedroom.

ONE OF THESE THINGS IS NOT LIKE THE OTHER

Shoving aside the maps, he laid his sweater down on the bed. He loosened his watch and dropped it into his chinos' pocket. He rolled up his sleeves. He shook his head and went back into the bathroom.

Squatting, he put his trembling hands on either side of the head. Blood dribbled down the neck. Jacob moved one hand under an armpit and supported the body's neck with the other. He tilted the body forward into a slumping, sitting position, shifting the weight back and forth gently until it sat upright. He wrapped a towel tightly around the bloody skull.

Grunting, he pulled the body by the arms out of the bathroom and into the closet. He leaned its back against the wall. He pushed the knees and feet closer in, and slid shut the louvered accordion door. Standing in front of the closed door, he nodded his head once.

How is this happening to me?

Jacob looked around the room. He scooped the clothes into the open suitcase. Returning to the bathroom, he washed his hands and inspected his pants for bloodstains.

Jacob froze. He stared straight in the mirror, eyes open wide. Hands dripping, he ran back into the room and yanked the curtains closed. He lifted one edge a fraction and peered out the window. Satisfied, he closed the curtains completely again and opened the door. He stuck his head out and looked up and down the empty hall. He closed the door.

Jacob sat on the edge of the bed. He licked his lips, looked at the phone on the bureau, and scowled. He stood, reached for the phone, froze. His hand jerked to the left and grabbed the room key off the nightstand. He spun around on the ball of his heel and walked out of the room, carefully hanging the Do Not Disturb sign on the door handle before taking off down the hallway.

Jacob squeezed behind a tall wire rack displaying pizza-flavored corn puffs and pressed against the pay phone.

"Holly. It's Jacob. Listen. I don't know if you'll check this or not before you get here. I tried paging you. You didn't answer. I've been loitering around inside this market for twenty minutes waiting for you to answer my page. I think the owner's going to call the cops if I hang out here any longer. Okay. I can't explain it all. You wouldn't believe me. But listen.

I know who the fake one of us is. It's Dallas. It's a long story. But listen. He's not us. And Ally is dead. Do you know Ally is dead? Did that sheriff get ahold of you? Holly, I don't know what to do. Something's happened. Listen. Meet me directly at Brett Ashley's. Get there as soon as you can. Do not go to the motel. Skip the motel and go straight to Gravesend, okay? Everything will make sense there. I'll call Brett and let her know."

Jacob pressed down the switch hook. He shoved his right hand in his trousers' pocket. He pulled out a Susan B. Anthony dollar and his watch.

"Damn!"

He patted the back pockets of his pants. He shoved a hand in each.

"Damn, my wallet!"

Jacob ran into the off-ramp intersection. He jerked to a stop and jumped back at the blaring horn of a car screaming past. He stepped back several paces and stood beside the curb. He wiped sweat off his upper lip and watched for a break in traffic.

He darted across the street, swung open the glass door of the motel, and made a beeline for the elevator.

"Mr. Barnes?" said a surprised man's voice.

Jacob stopped. He turned from the elevator. A blond man in a suit stood at the reception desk.

"That's his brother," said the desk clerk.

"Mr. Jacob Barnes?" He extended his open palm; Jacob nodded. The man looked apologetic. "I caught the family resemblance, and your brother told me about your black hair and all. I'm the sheriff of Clackamas County, Oregon. That covers Oregon City, where your father lived? And your brother was just out at? Have you received any of my messages?"

Jacob's eyes grew wide. "Yes."

The sheriff took a deep breath. "Well, let's go to your room, then." He glanced toward the girl behind the reception desk. "This is not the place."

Jacob nodded dumbly. Following the sheriff's extended arm, he walked into the elevator's open jaws.

Emerging on the floor, Jacob stared down the hall at the door to his brother's room. As they drew closer, he could see it was not closed completely.

"Looks like you left your door open," the sheriff noted.

Eyes wide, Jacob reached and grabbed the knob. He pressed his lips tight and opened the door a crack. He stuck his head in, gave the room a quick scan. The luggage and maps were all gone.

Jacob opened the door entirely. The sheriff followed him as they walked in.

Jacob nervously walked over to the closet, pulled the chair out from under the phone table, and sat down. He motioned for the sheriff to sit on the edge of the bed across from them. The sheriff sat and looked searchingly at Jacob. Jacob smoothed his pants legs.

"Mr. Barnes," said the sheriff.

Jacob looked at the sheriff, brow furrowed, mouth slightly open. "I appreciate your—concern—for my brother, but, still, I don't understand why you're here."

"To be honest with you, your brother's death makes your father's suicide start to look kind of fishy. But I've been keeping all this under my hat until I could talk to your brother directly. That's why I went and took some personal days and came out here on my own. I was aiming to talk to your brother before getting the Feds involved. Your brother that I met—the one who helped out with your father's death—he told me you all were all heading out this way."

The sheriff's smile betrayed a bashful note. "Mr. Barnes, your brother and I got to be pretty good friends while he was out in Oregon, so I'm taking a personal interest in this, as a friend."

Jacob shook his head. "So tell me what happened."

"Mr. Barnes," the sheriff said, "your brother's body—or what was left of it, if you'll pardon my saying—was found outside his cabin in Alaska."

Jacob blinked. He cocked his head, and his gaze drifted off, as if he were listening for something. He licked his lips, frowned, and put his hand to his mouth. Resting his palm against his chest, he straightened up in his chair.

"The Alaska State Troopers CIB contacted me trying to track down your brother's next of kin. Like I said, it made the suicide start to look a little fishy. Now, I didn't say anything to them about all that. I'm sticking my neck out coming here but—I care about your brother."

Jacob glanced at the closet where he'd hidden his brother's body. He caught himself looking and corrected his gaze to peer at the sheriff searchingly.

The sheriff clasped his hands together and cleared his throat. "A man had an appointment to visit your brother. He was going to buy some of his sled dogs. When he got there, it was quiet. He noticed there were no dogs. The kennel was open, and they'd all escaped. He went to the cabin to warn your brother. The heat had gone out, and the door was open and a window broken. The place had been vandalized real bad. A struggle had a taken place. An intense struggle."

He brought his hands to his chin and rested them there thoughtfully. He looked at Jacob, the floor, Jacob.

"Mr. Barnes. According to the officials in Alaska, your brother's attacker went and — there were remains found out with the dogs. Where they eat. Your brother's bloody clothes and his ID were sitting right on the kitchen table. Medical examiner hasn't made an exact match yet, but the body type and size he's been able to identify from the bones, and there's still hair samples — he's pretty certain it's your brother.

"I know your other brother, the Jake I know, was supposed to be up there, he bought tickets, but no one can confirm he was there yet. And no one can confirm exactly whose remains are there at the scene. Jake, that I know, he hasn't returned any of my calls or telegrams or emails since this happened."

"I got an email from him," Jacob said. "He said he wasn't going to Alaska after all. That he was just driving out. It sounded like he and Ally had had some sort of falling out."

"We don't know who did this. Like I said, there was an airship ticket to New York on his kitchen table, and some scribbled notes that didn't make much sense, but included the name of this motel and today's date."

Jacob's mouth opened slightly. His tongue moved about inside his mouth, as if tasting the air. He frowned, closed his eyes, shook his head, but took care to avoid looking at the closet.

The sheriff stood up and massaged his forehead. He sighed. "Maybe I should've called the Feds."

Jacob stood. "Excuse me," he said. He walked into the bathroom and soaked his face in cold water.

When he returned to the room, the sheriff was standing in front of the closet. He cleared his throat.

"Mr. Barnes, I'm going to need to see some ID, just to be safe here."

Jacob nodded. "Sure." He reached for his back pocket. "Oh! My wallet—it's in my sweater."

"Your sweater?"

"I sew inner pockets in my clothes. Pickpockets." He leaned to reach past the sheriff to the desk chair. "Um, excuse me."

"Oh. Sorry." The sheriff moved out of Jacob's way. The sweater was not on the back of the chair, or under the table.

"Huh." Jacob threw back the comforter. The bed sheets held nothing.

"Well, your brother was here last night. Someone slept here."

Jacob nodded. The sheriff opened the top two dresser drawers. "Nothing in here. Your brother travels light?"

"Ah—yes," Jacob said, watching the man's hands.

The sheriff whipped open the third drawer. He looked over at Jacob. "Nothing here." The sheriff looked up. "You check the closet?"

Jacob looked back at him.

"As my daughter would say—" The sheriff rolled his eyes. "DUH!" He gestured toward the closet door. "You mind, Mr. Barnes?"

"Of course."

Jacob walked over to the closet. Stiffly he grabbed the handle. The flimsy panels stuck. He yanked harder, and they folded open.

The closet was empty.

"Mr. Barnes, where is your other brother? The one who's staying in this room? Where are his things?"

Jacob stared at the empty closet floor. He kneeled and ran his fingers along the base of the wall inside the closet. It was slightly damp.

Jacob's gaze darted around the room. The sheriff scratched his head.

"Mr. Barnes, you know we're going to have to ask you about your whereabouts, and find your other brother. And find Jake—"

"Yes!" Jacob said with exasperation.

"Do you have any idea of anyone who might want to hurt your brothers, or you?"

Jacob's eyes opened wide. "I have no idea," he said through clenched teeth.

"We're missing something obvious," the sheriff said. "Some place we forgot to look." He looked around the room, settling at his feet. "Of course! The first place we should've checked for something missing." He got on all fours and lifted up the comforter, looking under the bed. Jacob stepped up close behind him.

"Yeah! There's something here!" the sheriff exclaimed. "I can almost reach it. Got it!"

The sheriff backed out from under the bed. Jacob slammed the tequila bottle against the back of his head. The sheriff fell to the floor. Jacob held his breath. *That sure was melodramatic.*

He watched the sheriff, motionless. He crouched beside him and felt his neck. "Thank God," he whispered, detecting a pulse.

He peeked under the bed to see what the sheriff had found. His hand was holding a keyring.

Damn!

Jacob pried the keys from the sheriff's hand. It was a thick bundle, greasy. Labeled unwisely, so any thief would know which was for "House" and "Garage." *Definitely Dal's*, Jacob thought.

He noticed the keyring: a portable flash drive made from purple translucent plastic.

Jacob grabbed the pager off his hip and plugged the drive into its data port. The pager's display lit up a list of file names; Jacob jiggled his thumb along a joystick to scroll through them:

abnormalities_home.xml
astounding_dr_cerebro.xml
cassandra_voices_LP.xml
freaks_sideshows_banners.xml
healers_occultists.xml
hyena_boy_bio.xml
images/
index.xml
invite_helping_hand.xml

living_skeleton_home.xml
lobster_family_home.xml
manimals_list.xml
poster_brother_barnes.xml
siamese_twin_love.xml
movie_womanN2ape.xml

He jerked the joystick back and double-jiggered it to select the file containing his name. The pager's offline web browser launched, displaying for Jacob a tiny image of a webpage. Jacob zoomed in and zig-zagged across the page, piecing together the total.

It was a scan of a cheaply printed, yellowing poster. It featured blocky capital letters and numerous starbursts. At the center of the poster was a man's crudely drawn figure. His arms stretched above his head, and a cape billowed behind him. His hair blew wild in the wind, and his eyes were extra-large, wide open, and red.

Jacob frowned. He squinted to read the poster's hand-drawn lettering, pixilated by the pager's poor resolution:

Come one come all! FAITH HEALING REVIVAL! This Sunday only! Come experience the Divine Ecstasy and Healing Spirit of God in Man!! Experience an afternoon of Power and Healing with BROTHER BARNES, World-Famous Spiritual Guide to Kings and Queens! Laying of the Hands! Music! Fellowship! Plus a special anointing by Jake, the amazing BOY-CHILD PROPHET. He's speaks of Times to Come, and his Touch cures your Ills!

On either side of the last paragraph were drawings of two small, red handprints.

Beneath the image of the poster, the owner of the site had added a caption: "This turned up among Bibles and anti-communist tracts at the estate sale of a widow in Walla Walla. I've never seen anything else for this act. If you have info or pieces in your collection, please contact me!—Erv Eckard, Circus Collectibles."

Jacob jerked the keyring out of the pager's port. He threw them both on the floor and stomped on each, shattering the devices against the motel carpet.

I'm no fucking circus act, Jacob thought. *This is not my family. This cannot be my family.*

Jacob sat down, pale and sweating. He looked at the sheriff, still unconscious. *Could I have been wrong about Dal?*

He could think of only one thing left to do. He pulled a piece of paper from his shirt pocket. He grabbed the phone and dialed.

"Mom?" he said. "I need to come home now."

GRAVESEND

Brett Ashley hung up her phone, setting the receiver gently in its cradle. *It stands to reason. My son would be the one who moved to New York. Who was drawn to this part of the country, drawn back east to the part of the country from where his ancestors came.*

Shivering, she drew her dressing gown close around her.

"Here he comes," she whispered. "He's coming back to me."

She turned and ascended the stairs to her bedroom, methodically stepping on one at a time. She rounded the landing. She pushed open the door to her bedroom and looked around until her gaze rested on the dressing table. She advanced inside, holding her eye in the mirror above it.

She sat on the cushioned bench, never breaking eye-lock with her own reflection. She turned her face from left to right, examining each profile. She sighed and looked away, surveying instead the items arranged atop the table: the ivory brush-and-comb set, the tiny tin pots of cosmetics, the baroque glass bottles of scent. One perfume bottle, cast in the shape of a dove, caught her eye. She touched its wings, remembering when he'd given it to her. Her lips pressed tight. Her dark brown eyes welled with tears; she wiped them away.

She shook her head. "No," she said firmly. "No." Louder. "Not this time. It's going to be all right this time."

She lifted her head with resolve and met her own eyes. She examined herself in the mirror and nodded.

He examined himself in the rearview as best he could, the car rattling along the dirt road. One hand gripping the wheel, he smoothed back his wet hair with the other, then inspected his palm for any residue of the black dye. Clean. He lifted his head and pointed his chin from left to right, scrutinizing his face in the mirror. He ran his fingers along his cheek, wincing from the fresh-shave sting.

He leaned back in his seat for a wider view of himself. He frowned and swayed to the left, looking instead in the driver's side mirror. *Objects in mirror are closer than they appear.*

Fuck yeah we are, he thought.

He picked a hair off his black sweater. He brushed clean the lap of his chinos.

Clearing his throat, he said aloud, "Oy." His voice was loud but tentative. "Oy!" he said asserting too much confidence this time, sounding more like a skinhead salute than Yiddish interjection. He cleared his throat again. "Oh-yee," he said, his tone curling and twisting. "Oy," he said. He shook his head, frowning. "Oy veh."

"Hello?" she said. "Please come in." She pressed her index finger against the intercom button. A loud buzz echoed down the hallway. She seated herself in a padded, high-back armchair. The front door clicked and creaked from the foyer.

Brett Ashley wore a pantsuit cut of neutral, stone-colored silk. The legs of the pantsuit flared slightly at the ankle. The pale tones made her dark brown eyes all the more powerful. The lines of her ensemble, strong yet reserved, bespoke understated authority and were adorned only by matching fabric-covered buttons and a single silver clasp. Another silver clasp adorned her long blonde hair, gathered to one side and falling in elegant waves down the other. Her eyebrows were the same blonde as her hair, unenhanced with pencil. She wore a thin bracelet of silver and opals, and matching drop earrings.

"I'm in the sitting room," she announced. She glanced at the end table next to her. Sitting up straight, she narrowed her eyes, facing forward. She tapped the manicured nails of her right hand on the tabletop.

Through the doorway a silhouetted figure approached, slowly working its way down the dark hall. The figure paused on the other side of the doorway, palms held aloft and floating forward through the air.

"Please come in," Brett Ashley said authoritatively.

ONE OF THESE THINGS IS NOT LIKE THE OTHER

He stepped into the cool yellow light of the parlor. She stifled a gasp. He froze. They stared at each other.

"It's me," he said. "I'm Jacob. The one from New York."

"Forgive me," she said, dumbstruck. "You do look so much like him." She shook her head, collected herself, and rose. She opened her arms, and they embraced.

She withdrew first. "And yet not like him," she said, looking him up and down. Her son nodded. He indicated his rumpled black sweater and chinos.

"Yes, ma'am," he said. "We've all struggled to try and make our own way."

"Please, sit down."

He perched on the edge of the fainting couch opposite her, sitting up straight.

"You color your hair," she noted.

Her son blushed. He ran his fingers through his tousled black curls. "Yes," he admitted. "We all did little things to ourselves. To look different."

Brett nodded. "Vanity. You *are* my son." She touched her right temple with her index finger. "And it appears you have my poor eyesight as well. I use contact lenses."

He removed the thick, black glasses. "They started going bad a couple of years ago. From all the reading and studying."

"Are you a student?"

"I'm in medical school," he said. "But I also have—personal studying. Spiritual. Ah, I'm converting to Judaism."

"I see." They nodded at each other. "Well, that would be a first for the family." She cleared her throat. She gestured to the finely appointed room about them. "And as you can tell," she sighed, "our family has been around for a while. This house dates from the Colonial era. We've lived here for generations. But it's only me, now."

She smiled grimly. "Sitting at this old table always makes me feel like I should be holding a séance. I always wondered if generations before us used this very table for such parlor games. Rappings, levitations, communications from the dearly departed. Although that's probably not the best idea, is it?"

He sputtered a small laugh. "Probably not. I think I'd be more interested in silencing the departed."

The sheriff drew a violent gasp. He opened his eyes.

Staggering, swaying, he picked himself up off the floor. He looked around the motel room with trepidation. He sat on the side of the bed. He checked his watch; a half hour had passed.

He grabbed the phone, his finger whipping around the dial. "Hey, it's me," he said, voice parched and thin. "Yeah, I know. Listen, I need an address. In Gravesend, New York. Yeah, Brooklyn. Sorry. Residential. The name is Brett Ashley."

"None of—" she gestured toward Jacob's hair, "—your changes have had any significant effect, have they? You may have come closer to yourself, but you're still no farther away from your father."

He sighed. "No." He leaned close, propping himself with one arm braced against the lip of the fainting couch. "You really understand everything."

"I've had a long time to contemplate...everything. And of course, yes, he speaks to me as well."

"Maybe it's not just him."

"Excuse me?"

Jacob looked away shyly. "I always talked to you. I mean, our mother, the woman who died. We used to tell each other how our lives would be different if she were alive. How she'd protect us from him. Maybe you must have felt me."

"I expect you're right," she murmured.

Jacob stood up and walked to the window. "Dad had buried his wife behind the house we were born in. Every time he moved us, we built a new grave back in the trees somewhere where he wouldn't see us. We made up this secret game. We told Dad we were playing Buried Treasure, but actually, every time we moved, we dug a new grave for Mom in the backyard. For me, that was for you. We'd bury flowers, pretty little rocks, bits of fruit, and pile a bunch of dirt on top and a big rock for a headstone. We held whole little mock funeral ceremonies. I wanted to keep her—you—near me."

Brett's eyes watered. She pressed her lips together. She turned away and stared into the cold fireplace.

"You must think me heartless," she said bitterly. "Knowing I've been alive all this time, but left my son trapped inside such a nightmare."

"No," Jacob said. "No."

"Let me tell you everything," Brett said, resting her hands

in her lap. "When I was young, I fell in love with a man. A disheveled, romantic young poet who gave readings at the local college. He soon abandoned the academy; I abandoned my family and its privilege. I thought it was all so daring, so brave, so beatnik-chic. We explored the country like vagabonds. I was often frightened—drugs, sex, police—things I'd only ever seen in movies. But somehow I thought I deserved it. They were lessons, no, punishments more accurately, which I deserved for my privileged upbringing. Sins of the fathers, you know.

"Of course we weren't married. We ended up living in what was called a 'commune,' a raggedy circle of trailers, wagons, vans, and school buses. More like gypsies, or a circus."

"Outside New Garton? On the Hermann Creek?"

"Yes, exactly." She shook her finger at him. "You've done your homework."

Jacob smiled thinly.

"My biggest fear then," she continued, "was that my social status would reveal itself. That my 'sisters' would exchange snobbish smirks when I lagged behind them shucking corn, my inexpert fumbling with the unfamiliar labor. It already took my every ounce of strength to have sexual relations with a strange new brother, to sip another bitter tea, to smile through beastly hallucinations everyone else found delightful. It was frightening, but I was desperately trying to be a good sport.

"Becoming pregnant was also frightening, yet not entirely without precedent. I'd encountered another expectant woman there, and met women with children already. They'd told me about that doctor and his wife offering secret care in New Garton, and how they'd nurse me afterward.

"When my boyfriend saw this beautiful boy, looking to him for life and love, howling hungry mouth and grabbing little hands, he dropped his renegade ideals like a hot coal. At the first opportunity when he and I were alone together, he asked, with the greatest delicacy, if I would consider asking my family for support. I informed him that the arrangements had already been taken care of. Some might call me ruthlessly practical, but I consider myself sensible, a survivor.

"I had already called my parents. I hadn't asked for money. I hadn't told them I was pregnant or where I was. I had merely warned them I would be needing their help. That we'd be coming home. We would come back and live with them. I knew my mother and the servants would help look after the child. My boyfriend would find a job, and we would eventually gain independence from my family.

"I rested for several days. We learned to handle our little handful. And just as my commune 'sisters' were losing interest in the novelty of a new child, we packed our van to head home. I was fearful of my future, yet also somewhat relieved. Frankly, I felt as if my life was now finally taking its proper course. We'd sown our wild oats. We'd proven our individuality, rebelled against our families, and now it was time to return home and settle down."

He paused his car at the corner and looked in both directions. Waiting for a car to pass, he checked his hair in the rearview again and attempted to flatten the black, curly locks into submission. He growled in frustration.

A sign on the corner read: No Horn Honking $350 Fine. He laughed and pounded his fist on the horn, blaring it as he tore through the intersection.

"Here I come, Momma!" he called out.

"We left at night," Brett related, speaking slowly and carefully, opening a long-sealed trunk of memories. "We headed out of town on one of those dark Texas highways. We'd been on the road only a half hour or so when a pickup truck blazed past us. I remember my boyfriend said, 'Finally! That fellow's been following us ever since we left!'

"Soon there was a blinding light. The truck had driven on ahead of us, past a bend in the road, then stopped and turned around, facing us, with its lights off. Once we got too close, it had turned them on. My boyfriend threw on the brakes, and our van spun out of control, tumbling off the side of the road. We were fortunate not to tip over. My boyfriend asked if we were okay. I said I thought so, but I had my hands full trying to quiet your cries. He stormed outside to confront the truck driver. I assume they got into some sort of a disagreement, but I couldn't hear clearly over your crying.

"There was a loud noise. A thump. On the windshield."

Brett held her hand, fingers outstretched, in the air before her. Her lips parted, but she did not speak for several long, creeping seconds.

"I looked up," she finally said. "I saw my boyfriend's head roll down the windshield. I screamed. And the side of the van, the door, ripped open. Jake Barnes stood in the open door, wide-eyed and horrible, the truck's lights bathing him like some Goya painting. I thought we were going to die. He climbed in. I threw myself at him. All I could think of was keeping him away from my son. He hit me. Later they told me it was the butt of a gun. I awoke in the clinic. I had been unconscious for days.

"But, all that time, I'd had no escape, no relief. I had been dreaming. I was alone in some dark space, and a dim light grew over a nearby ridge. A figure would slowly appear climbing over it. It was Jake Barnes, lit from behind in an unearthly red glow. He held my boyfriend's head in his hand. He held it high like a lantern, and a dull yellow light seeped from the eyes and mouth. The head spoke. My boyfriend spoke to me, but not with his voice. It was Jake's. He said that he had my boy, and that I was not to speak a word of it. My boy was his now. If I ever came after him, he would bring me my son's head.

"That vision was fresh in my mind when I awoke in the clinic. They told me they'd found my boyfriend's body. They never said anything about my son, and neither did I. I told them it had been dark, that I'd never seen my assailant. That midwife, she came to see me. She asked, carefully, what had happened to my child. I told her I didn't know anything. She told me a local man had recently lost his wife in childbirth. She described him: tall, flaming red hair, wild eyes, thick red beard. She watched for my reaction, but I gave her none, although it was of course a face I'd never forget. The face you try now to obscure. I told her that part of my life was over. I told her I was going home as soon as I felt better. She left. And I did."

Brett wiped her eyes, cleared her throat. "I never told my parents the details. I think they were actually relieved I came home free from the complications of an unwed lover and a bastard child. Our doctor could tell I'd given birth, but no one spoke of this directly. I received a limitless supply of pretty blue-and-yellow tranquilizers, and a charming psychiatrist who never made me talk about anything too specific.

"You see, I wanted this house. I wanted furniture and

money, delicacies to eat, perfumed baths to savor. I got them.
And I kept my mouth shut. I was eventually accepted again
into society, within limits. No one believed my parents' Siam
story, I'm sure. But by that point I was only interested in
becoming the safe and comfortable spinster that I am today.

"But I did not forget. The dreams from Jake continued
sporadically, but they were lectures more than images. He
would describe scenes of your growing up. Once or twice
every year. He would talk about holding one of you on his lap,
feeding you raw venison he'd shot and butchered himself.
He'd describe one of you, so well behaved and patient, waiting
for your turn at a wooden table in some log cabin far removed
from civilization. Once, he said he had an older Mexican girl
from a nearby town help take care of you. He teased me that
she was your wet nurse, but then contradicted himself, saying
he wouldn't let her hold you."

"You're right," Jacob said. "For years he hired local girls to
help out. Always girls."

"He gloated," she said. "Told me I wouldn't recognize my
own child because he'd made them all look like himself. Tell
me, what did your father say in his suicide note?"

Expressionless, Jacob quoted the email. "'I'm going to
leave this world, and yours will fall apart.'"

"Yes, that sounds correct. Jake felt he created you, and that
he was the glue holding you boys' world together, even after
you stopped living with him.

"Jacob, the dreams from Jake actually encouraged me. You
see, I hired a private detective. I kept tabs on you. Occasionally
I'd lose track, but I'd have you found again. Your father was a
creature of habit."

"But he's not my father."

She shook her head sadly. "You can never escape him, no
matter from where your genes come. You can never purge him.
You can diversify yourself, you can explore your history, but
expanding your idea of yourself will only complement his
presence, not dilute it. You have to embrace it ultimately, make
it yours, turn him into an asset instead of an enemy."

Goddammit! The sheriff glared at the traffic around him. *Why
the hell didn't I bring a magnetic strobe, or at least a siren?*

He slammed his fist on the dashboard of the rental car. He

winced and held his hand horizontal before his face. His fingers shook.

Dammit, Jake, I'm coming. I'll be there fast as I can. Daddy's coming to get you.

Brett Ashley folded her hands together diplomatically. She drew a deep breath.

"I did come for you once. I knew where you were at that service station. I took my parents there, on one of our last holidays together. I convinced them a mountain tour would be rustic. We spent the nights at hunting lodges. During the day we took scenic drives.

"I drove them to your service station. On our first visit, the old man served us, but as he was plugging the charger into our vehicle, I glimpsed one of you playing out in the fields behind. So I drove in a great circle for an hour, finally coming back. My parents didn't even notice.

"This time, one of you came out. The sun was blazing on your red hair like spun gold, fiery silk. Your big ears were red and pink with the light shining through them. You wore blue coveralls smeared with oil and dirt. Your freckled forearms were burned pinkish red.

"You stuck the plug into our Airstream, which took a long time to charge. I came out and asked you if you could show me the ladies room. We stood face-to-face, staring. Sweat beaded across your forehead, trickling down your sunny brow. You licked your full lips, and nodded. I followed you into the garage. No one else was there. You were still bright red, even once inside the dark garage. You were blushing. You opened the door of the restroom and stepped inside to turn on the light. I followed you, not really thinking. We were both transfixed.

"You said, 'Here you go, ma'am.' Your voice had a lilt of the South in it, but you nodded your head with a quick, self-conscious jerk I'd seen my mother do thousands of times.

"I said, 'Thank you,' and kissed your cheek. I—embraced you. As if it were the most common thing in the world, as if that were what one always did to express gratitude to servicemen.

"You didn't resist me. You were stiff for a moment, as if uncertain of what was happening. Momentarily I feared you would think I was seducing you. But suddenly you gasped once, twice, then fell into me. You cried like a baby. I held you like my baby. You could have been.

"I don't know how long we stood like that.

"Then, the rest of you came. I heard quite a ruckus outside. Your brothers were playing some game. You ran out of the garage and yelled to take it out back—you had customers. I never saw you all, just heard your shouts and running feet. When I came out of the garage, you were back at the power plug. I climbed in the driver's seat. You didn't even look at me as I paid you. When we drove off, I could see you in my mirror, standing practically in the middle of the road, watching me leave.

"I drove as fast as I could to the nearest motel, checked my parents and I into separate rooms—despite their complaints over the shoddiness of the accommodations. I booked our return flights and called for the nearest place to return the Airstream. When I got home, I fired my investigator.

"It hurt too much. It hurt more than anything. More than losing you, more than seeing my man killed, more than the nightmares of your father. It was excruciating. I never attempted to find you or contact you again, but I want you to know I did, once.

"But that wasn't you I met, was it?"

He shook his head. "I'm sorry. I know which of us it was, though."

"Did he tell you all? Did he brag about some strange woman making a pass at him?"

"No. He only told me something recently. All he told me was that he remembered his mother holding him. None of the rest of us remembers that, so I thought he was lying. Then I thought he must be the fake one, the other boy. Miss Ashley, there's a lot I have to tell you."

He crept up the steps of the porch on tiptoe. His view through the glass of the front door was obscured by the white lace curtains on the other side of the glass. He could only make out a dim hallway, with light coming through a doorway at the far end.

He bent over and pressed his ear to the glass and listened.

Frowning, he stood and looked over each shoulder. The street was empty and still—no cars, no neighbors. Clouds hung low and gray. The dual chirps of a bobwhite's song cut the silence: a long, low note and a short, higher one separated by a pregnant, wary pause.

A jarring clang rang through the house. Brett and her son looked at each other, startled.

"I'm not expecting anyone," she said. "Please excuse me while I take care of this." She rose and stepped into the dark hall, shutting the parlor door behind her.

He bent over on the fainting couch, head in his hands. At the sound of voices from the hall, he bolted upright and cocked his head toward the door. Hands balled into fists, he retreated from the door until he was backed against the parlor's far wall. He stared at the closed door. Voices quieted. Footsteps approached. The door cracked open.

Brett stepped into the room, ashen. She rushed from the door and recoiled against the wall opposite him.

"What is it?" he asked her.

The door opened again. A true duplicate entered the room: black hair, black sweater, chinos. He took a step forward. "Don't trust him," he said. "Don't believe a word he says."

Brett cleared her throat. "I don't know what to believe at the moment," she said, her voice acquiring a commanding edge. "Young man, please, go stand over there by him." She gestured across the room.

The two men eyed each other with furious, blazing eyes but moved side by side. Brett stepped in front of the parlor door, hand resting for support on a wood curio cabinet. She narrowed her eyes at them.

"Very clever," she murmured. "You dye your hair, get glasses and such to differentiate yourself, but you can still mimic each other when you want to. Play 'Guess Who?'"

"I don't know what the hell is going on here," said the boy on the right.

"Sure you do," snapped the other.

"He's dyed his hair to look like me," sputtered the first.

"That's absurd. I don't have to pretend to be anything. You're the one here trying to make her believe you, not me, Glowie."

Brett snapped to attention. "Glowie—that's the one in Hollywood, right?"

"We don't use those old names anymore—there's proof right there he's not me, not Jacob."

Brett's face clouded in concentration. "But you do, too. I remember hearing that name when I talked to one of you on the phone before, but I can't remember whom it was—Jacob or one of the others."

The boys glared at each other. Both raised hands to run through their black hair, but stopped upon seeing the other's mirroring motion. Spitefully, the one on the right finished his original gesture.

"All right," Brett called out. "Let's aim for something simple. Why does it matter which of you is which?"

"Because he's a killer!" the left-side brother blurted. "He's turned against us. He's the one from Hollywood, the gay one. He went up and killed our brother in Alaska! There's a sheriff from Oregon who knows all about it! He tore Ally to pieces!"

Brett's eyes remained steely.

"You did that, and you know it," the other said. "Now you're trying to pretend you're me."

"That's not all. Then he killed my other brother in his hotel room. He wants to kill all of us, and you can't let him. He doesn't want to be Jake Barnes. He wants to be your son. He wants to get rid of all of us and start over as someone new."

"I didn't kill Dal! It was an accident; he fell. He slipped on a banana latte."

Brett raised an eyebrow. "No one could make *that* up."

One brother crossed in front of the other. They paced circles around each other. Brett squinted at the boys, following them as they sparred.

"Brett. You warned me things could get dangerous," said one. "Dal, our brother from Texas. We got in a fight at his motel here. He hurt his head and died. But it was an accident."

"An accident!" said the other, facing his brother. "We were just fighting, like any brothers. Just friendly. It was an accident. But then I went to go make a call and—this one must've been there at the motel; he must have been spying on us the whole time. Because while I left the—"

"No, it wasn't, you killed him!" said one.

"No, you're the murderer!" said the other. "You got into the motel room and took the body. He must have told the receptionist girl he was me, or our brother. He hid the body—"

"That's why the door was open!"

"And stole my ID! That's how you can tell who is who! The one with Jacob Barnes' ID is the killer. He's not me, the one with my ID."

"That's a convenient situation," Brett snapped. "I'm going to take a wild guess neither of you have ID."

"He stole it!"

"He stole it!"

"Yes," she said, nodding. She glared at them. "You say the Alaskan brother was dismembered?"

"Yes," said the other. "He killed him, then fed him to the dogs."

Brett winced. "Wait," she said. "Your Alaskan brother was killed and—" she swallowed "—disposed of? You said he was unrecognizable?"

Both men nodded.

"And you say your brother from California did this?"

"Yes!" they said in unison. "Him!"

Brett shook her head, waving her hands angrily in front of her face. "How do you know who was the killer and who the victim? The Alaskan brother could've killed the Californian, and the Texan, and is now in disguise as the New Yorker. How do we know who killed whom in Alaska?"

The men blinked at each other.

"No," one said, shaking his head, fighting tears. "Ally wouldn't do that. He's—he's the most gentle of all of us. He never hurt anyone. He was scared of people. He lived alone."

"No!" said the other. "He acted that way, but he was just as shrewd and ruthless as the rest of them!"

"He couldn't have done it, but you could have!" He pointed at the other man. "Brett, he's a complete hedonist. No morals. He lives in Hollywood, he's gay, he goes to orgies, he does drugs. I've heard all about it. That's probably what started this, paranoia or hallucinations or something. When was the last time you slept, Hollywood boy? How much GHB are you taking? Or is it crystal meth you like?"

Brett faced the boys, silent and expressionless, her fingertips resting on the drawer handle of the end table.

One Jacob put his hands on his hips. "I get it now! That's why you still use those old names with each other, those pet names. Brett, those were our secret names. Dad didn't know about them and wouldn't let us use them. I couldn't figure out why anyone would want to keep using secret, childhood names when we're adults, and our father was dead. But something happened today that made me think about what sort of people like keeping secrets. What sort of people get a thrill from the forbidden, from subterfuge.

He folded his arms across his chest, triumphant. "What happened up in Alaska was a lover's quarrel, wasn't it? That's what was going on. That's what's been going on for years, isn't it? Ally's gay, too—and Holly, he was your lover!"

"That's enough!" Brett aimed a small pistol at one brother. "That's quite enough. Of everything. Jacob, come stand by your mother."

Both boys moved to join her. Brett jabbed the pistol toward the closest boy. "Not you," she warned.

"What?" he said.

The other boy raced to her side. "Thank God," he gasped.

The boy who was the gun's target flustered wildly. "I'm not—What are you doing? It's not me. It's him. He'll probably kill you next!"

Brett shook her head slowly. "I may just be getting to know you boys," she said, glaring down the sights of her pistol. "But I already know my family. I know my blood. And what you have suggested goes too far."

She cocked the gun. "No son of mine would ever even dream of such a story."

She fired, hitting him cleanly in the forehead. He fell to the floor, a stunned look on his face.

"There are some things a mother just knows," she said quietly.

The sheriff paused his car at the corner, looking in both directions. He noticed a street sign: No Horn Honking $350 Fine. He shook his head. "Damn, boy, where the hell are you?"

Brett turned. "You said police are already involved?"

He nodded.

"Then let's work fast. You create some disarray in here. I'll go to the kitchen and get a knife."

He looked at her quizzically.

"To put in his hand."

He nodded and turned to the door.

"Oh, and son," she held up her hand and smiled. "Then we have to sit down and get our stories synchronized, yes? You have to be strong now. The one who dies, the accident at the motel—you say this one took the body?"

"Yes, ma'am."

"Any idea where?"

"No, ma'am."

"So his prints and fibers should be all over the body. I've seen all the shows on television. He could just as well have killed him, yes? There was nothing about the death to definitely tie it to you, was there?"

He shook his head.

"Good," she said. She embraced him. "It's time to be strong. It's time to be a man."

She smiled sadly and stroked his sable hair. "Once all of this is done, maybe we can be whatever's left of a family."

He nodded.

"Now let's get to work," she said, wiping her tears. "That sheriff you mentioned could find his way here soon."

"Huh?"

"The sheriff you said was looking into all this."

"Yeah." He scratched the back of his neck, squinting. "The sheriff." He nodded. "We should call the local police, too."

Brett looked at him with alarm.

"Once we get everything set up. It'll look less suspicious if we call the local police and tell them our story."

"Yes."

"Let me know when you're ready, and I'll call." He put his hand to his stomach and scowled. "But I need to go to the bathroom first."

Brett nodded soberly. She gestured toward the stairs. He climbed them, found it, and locked the door behind him.

Secreted in the bathroom, he leaned close to the door and opened his mouth. He cupped his hands around his lips and gagged loudly. He retched awfully but produced no bile, not even saliva, just noise. He moaned loudly.

Then he turned to the sink and turned on the hot water. He threw open the shower curtain and searched through the soaps and glass vials of bath beads. Frowning, he opened the mirrored wall cabinet and surveyed the faded tins and bottles. The top drawer of a marble-topped antique vanity behind him proved more fruitful. He smiled and pulled out a woman's pink razor. He rifled further through the drawer until he found a pair of hair-cutting scissors.

Holding them both, he faced the mirror, steam rising from the basin. He shut off the water, wiped the mirror clear, and smiled approvingly at his reflection.

"How about a makeover?" he said wryly.

The car crept into the cul-de-sac, stopping before a large, Dutch Colonial farmhouse. Its white clapboards contrasted with the black tree limbs spidering around the house.

The sheriff shut off his engine.

The house had a small wooden front porch, held in by four thin white wooden columns. Thick, overhanging eaves sloped to a point over the porch. Two windows peered out from the black-shingled roof.

The sheriff peered back. There was no motion on the porch or in the upper windows. Curtains occluded the downstairs windows, as well as those on the side addition.

He squinted at the address. He nodded and squeezed the door handle.

Brett pressed the knife-grip against the still fingers, her own hand shrouded in a lace doily. She laid the weapon to rest beside the boy's body. She stood. She shook her head, looking up at the ceiling, listening to the sounds of her son's sickness. She took a deep breath and reached, trembling, for the phone. She lifted the handset as if it was made of stone, and raised it to her ear and cleared her throat. She reached to dial.

She paused, cocking her head at a soft crunching sound outside. She set down the phone and ran to the window. Squinting, she peered through small holes in the lace curtains. She ran to the front door.

The sheriff cautiously clicked his car door shut. He stepped into the street, crouching slightly, and crept toward the house.

The front door flew open. Brett emerged onto the porch. She closed the door quickly behind her.

"Who are you?" she demanded, shooting him a withering

glare from atop the porch.

The sheriff straightened. Extending his hand, he walked over to her. "It's okay," he said, "I'm police."

Brett looked at him, his rental car. The sheriff smiled and pulled out his wallet. "Are you okay?" he asked, flashing a badge.

Brett looked at the badge, then met the sheriff's eyes. Her face crumbled.

"It's horrible!" she gasped, falling forward. "So horrible!"

He rushed forward to catch her, and she sobbed into his chest. "I can't believe it," she choked. "It's too much."

"Where is he?" The sheriff wrapped his arm protectively around her.

She looked up at him, sniffing. "He's — dead." She wiped tears from her cheeks and looked back at the house. "He tried to kill his, his — brother — and me."

The sheriff drew her closer. Carefully he guided her, step-by-step, up into the house. He reached for the door handle and looked down at her. She nodded.

Creaking, the door swung open into the silent house. No noise came from the bathroom upstairs. The sheriff and Brett stepped into the foyer. He shut the door behind them.

"He's probably in the sitting room," she whispered, "with the other one." He nodded soberly, and they shuffled together down the dark hall.

He jumped slightly at the sight of the body. "That's Jacob," he said, "The one from New York."

Brett shook her head sadly. "No," she whispered. "It's the one from Alaska. He disguised himself as Jacob after he killed the others."

The sheriff scowled. "Alaska?"

"You're here!" came a shout from the stairs behind them. Brett and the sheriff spun around.

He descended the stairs into the room: head shaved bald, five o'clock shadow trimmed into a thin strip of beard, a small gold earring clipped to one ear. He still wore the chinos but had lost the black sweater, was now wearing only a tight white T-shirt. He rushed across the room and threw his arms around the sheriff.

"Thank God you're here," Jake cried.

He hugged the sheriff tight, then kissed him full on the

lips. The sheriff held tense. Jake opened his eyes, smiling wide, eyes searching the man's face. The sheriff relaxed into the kiss, wrapping his arms around Jake and clutching him.

"Oh my god," Brett hissed acidly. She scowled at the two men kissing. She looked at the corpse on the floor. "Oh my god," she whispered. She put her hand over her eyes and collapsed onto the fainting couch.

The sheriff pulled from the kiss, hands laced together, cupping Jake's ass. "What happened here?" he said, eyes wet with relief.

Jake gulped. He licked his lips. He looked over at Brett on the couch. Her hands fell to her side. She narrowed her eyes at Jake, slowly shaking her head.

"It's been so awful," Jake sniffed. "Alaska attacked me when I went up there. He, he—"

Jake glanced at Brett, his lips curling at the corners almost imperceptibly. "He tried to rape me. I fought back—it was self-defense! He got hurt in our fight. Bad. I just—I just left him there. I didn't know what else to do. I didn't feed him to the dogs. I was in shock. They must have got loose somehow and turned on him. He probably trained them to attack people to begin with."

"No," the sheriff said, pulling the boy close again. "My boy. It's okay. I'm here now."

Jake looked over his shoulders at Brett. Their eyes locked.

"Mother called and told me who I really was, and that the Jake Barnes boys couldn't be trusted. She told me not to go to the motel but to come right here."

Brett broke his gaze and stared in defeat at the body on the floor.

Jake continued. He pulled away from the sheriff and walked over to the body. "Jacob came here a little while ago. He was insisting he was Brett's son, that I was going to try to kill Mother."

He looked at Brett, eyes wet. "He told her stories—that I'd killed Ally on purpose, and that I'd killed Dal as well at the motel. Is that true?" he asked the sheriff. "Are they all dead?"

The sheriff nodded grimly. "I'm afraid so. I know you didn't do it. They did it to each other. They did it to themselves."

"Jacob came here and tried to do it to me. He came at me

with that knife, but Mother saved my life."

The sheriff knelt beside Brett. "Is that right, ma'am? That doesn't sound quite like what you told me."

Brett looked up past the sheriff's shoulder at Jake. With resignation she tucked her hair behind her left ear, revealing a small birthmark. "Yes," she said quietly, "that's exactly what happened."

Jake sighed. He lowered his head. "Jake Barnes did this. He killed himself, and we all fell apart, turned on each other. He knew we'd fall apart without him."

The sheriff stood and took Jake's face in his hands. "You got a new daddy now."

The sun was setting low in Gravesend, orange blocks of light reaching across Brett Ashley's front porch. The sheriff and a local detective, in matching brown suits and dark sunglasses, stood on the porch behind crime-scene tape.

"I can't tell you how much I appreciate this." The sheriff clasped his hand on the detective's shoulder.

"I can't believe you got yourself into this," the detective whistled. "Damn, I thought you'd moved out west to simplify things. This is messier than anything you and I ever got into."

"I know. But he's a good boy. A good boy a lot of bad things have happened to. I think I can help him. I think we can be happy together."

"Well, that's all I ever wanted for you," the detective said, shaking his head. "I'll do all I can to keep everything to a minimum, but, you know, this is a bizarre crime. There's gonna be a serious investigation, and the media's going to go crazy."

The sheriff drew in a sharp breath. "I know. And you gotta do your job."

"Good thing no one ever knew about you and me. I should be able to reassure the investigators, keep things from going too far. I can help with that, but you're on your own with the media."

The sheriff nodded. "My place back home has a big fence around it. And his dad's place—hell, you can't even find the damn thing if you don't know about it."

The detective's partner joined them on the front porch. The sheriff and the detective moved a foot farther apart.

His partner cleared his throat. "She's sleeping now. The

boy's watching her. They're still working inside. Has the coroner gone?"

The detective and sheriff nodded.

"We got another message from the girlfriend down in Texas," his partner said. "She'll be up tomorrow to ID the body we found behind the motel."

"Did you interview the boy?" the detective asked his partner.

"Yes," the partner said, pulling out his notebook. The detective held out his hand.

"I'll take a look at your report and see how it compares with his story." His partner put away the notebook. The men nodded at each other.

HOME LAND

The sheriff lifted the quilt and slipped in beside Jake. Firelight shadows flickered their way from downstairs up into the loft of the Oregon cabin. He slid his arm around Jake, fingering smooth white skin and strands of hair.

"Nice you stopped shaving your chest," he murmured with appreciation.

Jake lolled over onto his side. "Glad you like it." He smiled slyly, sliding his knee up between the sheriff's thighs. His dick stiffened against his own thigh. His kneecap rested just below the sheriff's balls.

"Getting out of Hollywood's been good to you. You're a lot stronger, more confident. Lost some of that flab. You look more like a real man, less like the cityboy I first met. And I like your real eyes better than those contacts. So dark and beautiful."

Jake nuzzled against his throat. "It feels good just to be myself."

"You feel pretty good to me, too," the sheriff chuckled, stroking Jake's ribs. "Good to have someone to come home to again." A look of concern flickered across his face. "But if it's hard for you—being back in this town, in this house—"

Jake shook his head. He ran fingers along the side of the sheriff's ear, up into his thin, yellow hair. "No—I don't want to run from my past anymore. I want to take control—make it over for me, in my life, my image."

The sheriff nodded. "Tough boy," he murmured and kissed Jake. He nudged his hips forward, grinding his cock against the boy's. He chuckled, almost a growl, from a low place deep in his throat, rumbling from down around the depths of his esophagus.

Jake sighed loudly and flipped over, turning from the man. "Of course, making over this town could be a lot of work," he grumbled. He reached behind and snatched his pillow, cramming it up against his chest, wrapping his arms around it tightly.

"What's going on?" the sheriff asked with concern. He snuggled up behind and rested his head on Jake's shoulder, gazing in close-up at faint shadows of freckles. The sheriff frowned: there seemed to be fewer of the red marks.

"Oh," Jake snapped, "that lady at the tavern gave me attitude. Wouldn't let our hands touch when she gave me change. Were people here that freaked out by Dad?"

"That blonde lady? The young one?"

Jake nodded.

The sheriff sighed with relief, his body relaxing against the boy's body. "Oh, I wouldn't worry about her—or the rest of this town. Listen, son, I have a confession to make, as long as we're talking about your dad and all this."

Jake didn't move. "What?"

The sheriff sat up in bed, quilt falling off his chest and into his lap. He leaned back against the cabin wall, facing forward and staring off into the darkness of the rafters. He made a mental note to build a railing across the edge of the loft.

"What?" Jake repeated, voice betraying a new note of concern. He rolled over and looked up at his lover.

The sheriff folded his arms across his chest. "Your dad—yeah, he was a crazy old coot, but people weren't really afraid of him. They just thought he was a harmless loony. I'm sorry, but it's true."

Jake frowned. "Well, they didn't know the truth. You did. You knew what he was really like. What he could really do."

The sheriff glanced at Jake. He cringed sheepishly, nodding. "I know I told you how people kept clear of him," he said. "I know I said how he knew things, how he helped me solve that murder..." He trailed off, licking his lips and staring into the space where Jake Senior had ended his life. *Crazy old fuck,* the sheriff thought. *Time to free this boy from that old bastard's spell.*

Jake nudged him from his reverie. "Yeah...?"

"Well," the sheriff said, "I was exaggerating a bit." He rested a hand on the back of Jake's neck.

Jake's eyes narrowed. "How *much* were you exaggerating?" he queried the older man, a glint of caution sparking behind his dark eyes.

The sheriff shook his head slowly. "Ah—all the way. None of that happened."

"What do you mean?" Jake sat up.

"Look." He slid his palm down to Jake's chest, fingertip circling around a nipple, toying with soft tufts of hair. "You were so determined, talking about your Dad and his magic powers and everything. If I didn't match your stories, if I'd just nodded my head, you wouldn't have thought I really believed you. And I wanted you to. To be honest, I was really just thinking about getting into those tight jeans of yours."

Jake blinked. His jaw clenched. He swallowed. "I remember," he said quietly. "Me, too. So none of that happened?"

"What?"

"My dad. Showing you who killed that girl."

The sheriff slouched back down beside Jake. He rested his head on the pillow. The loft had grown dark, firelight fading. The sheriff couldn't see Jake's face flush or the sweat on his forehead. "I know it's hard to hear, son, but your dad was actually kind of a laughingstock around here."

"Then why does that lady at the tavern give me such grief?" Jake asked crossly. He rolled over, away from the sheriff.

The sheriff sighed with fond affection. "Well, I'm afraid that's a different matter. She's a little, well, jealous."

"What?"

"She and I used to have a thing going on. Not too serious, but it went on longer than it should've. I didn't get the balls to cut it off until you came along. Anyhow, she knows what's up with us. Probably jealous of you a bit."

"You and her?" Jake's face brightened. "You mean you didn't come out until you met me?"

The sheriff hit him with his pillow. "Don't flatter yourself, boy," he laughed. "I told you I played for both teams, back on our first night." He pressed in close beside Jake, his lips brushing against his ear.

"Remember, boy?" He whispered hotly, voice sinking low.

"Remember how much you liked me talking about fucking pussy? Talking about pussy with my dick up your ass?"

"I gotta pee," Jake croaked, words snagging in his suddenly dry throat. He lifted himself from the bed, moving cautiously toward the wall, arms outstretched, one step at a time in the dark loft. The sheriff watched him, following his silhouette, seeing enough to discern the flopping dick.

Feeling the cabin's wall with one hand, Jake descended the stairs. He turned the corner, deep dark now that the fire had died to embers. He eased shut the bathroom door behind him. With great care, he silently locked the latch. He yanked the string and the overhead bulb burned yellow. He stepped over to the sink and faced the mirror, examining himself. Jake Barnes, today.

His chest hair was coming in all right, but it was a pure thin blond, not the old orange curls. Jake already knew the color change of his eyes had precious little to do with contact lenses. The eyes of all the brothers had been uniformly green. But now his were brown, dark and secretive. He ran his fingers along his emergent ribcage. The weight loss had wrought a subtle sharpening of his facial features as well, drawing into focus his brow and jaw and chin. They jutted forth, asserting themselves, announcing their presence to the world. Conversely, the freckles were fading, bringing an evenness to his skin, a sameness, an advancing uniformity. Jake leaned in to the mirror. The one exception to his uniform, pale skin was a small birthmark below his left ear. He nodded slowly. He dug his fingers into his hair and held a fistful aloft, the newly limp locks not springing back as he was used to. He examined the blond roots. No dye needed this time.

"It's her," he whispered. "With all of them gone, I'm turning into her. Mother."

Jake returned to bed, slipping in alongside his man. He felt the sheriff's breath rise and fall beside him—life, in its simplest expression. Rise, fall. In, out. Breathing, fucking. So easy to do. So easy to make happen. So easy to extinguish. A man, men, a family. A town, a nation?

"Hey," he whispered aloud, even though he knew the man was asleep. "You know...it gets kind of lonely here sometimes, while you're at work."

Jake spoke to the dark, the fire's coals having burnt to ash

ONE OF THESE THINGS IS NOT LIKE THE OTHER

and the night lacking a moon.
   "I thought maybe we could get some dogs."

Born in Waco, Texas, D. Travers Scott was raised in wildly varying locations and conditions, from poolside caviar to mobile homes without running water. A born-again Southern Baptist and neopagan teen psychic, his eclectic childhood fueled his diverse adult explorations of sex, storytelling, and masculinity. He is the author of the acclaimed novel *Execution, Texas: 1987*, and has appeared everywhere from *Harper's* to *This American Life*. Currently he is pursuing a PhD in political communication. More information is available at his website: www.dtraversscott.com.